The Honor of a Highlander

A Novella

By:

April Holthaus

Cover design by April Holthaus

Printed in the United States
First Printing: September 2013
Edited by:
Sue Soares and Helen Nazzaro
ISBN-10: 1492221600
ISBN-13: 978-1492221609

Dedicated to:

My husband, for all of your love and support
and believing in me.

Laird Rory MacKinnon sets out to join William Wallace after discovering an imminent threat that the English have planned an attack. Raised as a warrior, he has given his heart and soul to fight for Scotland's freedom, until he meets a lass who has captured his heart like no other, Lady Annella. After a brutal attack on her land, Rory discovers that Annella has been taken prisoner by the English. Now Rory must fight; not only to secure his own clan's freedom but to save the woman he loves.

Annella, the eldest daughter of the MacCallum clan vows to never marry, until the day Rory MacKinnon enters her life and opens her heart. Heading off to war she knew they had no future. After her father offers aid to Laird MacKinnon and his men to help in their campaign, her castle is attacked and her father is killed by the English for treason. Starved and beaten for denying her allegiance to the English King, Annella has earned her place in the gallows. Her fate now rests in Rory's hands.

Contents

Chapter 1...6
Chapter 2...24
Chapter 3...39
Chapter 4...51
Chapter 5...62
Chapter 6...72
Chapter 7...84
Chapter 8...98
Chapter 9...110
Chapter 10...121
Chapter 11...132
Chapter 12...143
Chapter 13...154
Chapter 14...168
Chapter 15...185

Chapter 1

Late August
Argyll, Scotland 1297

"Bollocks," Annella cried out after pricking her finger with the needle again. This was her third time having to repair her blue and green *arisaid*.

Berta cleared her throat and gave Annella a solemn look of disappointment. "That is no' a way for a lady to speak."

Annella peered up at Berta and gave her a sour expression when she was not looking.

"How did ye ruin yer plaid this time?"

"I dinna ruin it, it ripped while I was riding up the hill. It got snagged on a tree branch," she replied with a dreadful look upon her face, waiting for one of Berta's never-ending lectures. Berta had been her maid ever since she was a wee lass and had a history of being short-tempered.

"After ye get done, there will be nothing left of it. Come now, lass, ye must get dressed and fix that unruly hair of yers. Yer father has visitors coming today and he is expecting ye to be down in the great hall." She walked over to the wooden chest at the end of the bed and pulled out a fresh chemise and gown. "I will fix yer plaid while ye get dressed."

With a dreadful look on her face, she slowly got up and took her time dressing. *Another suitor?* Even the thought of it made her stomach cringe. Over the past several months, her father had invited suitors for her to meet in hopes that she would agree to marry one of them without dispute.

Laird Stewart, the last man who came, smelled vile and was much older than Annella. She could still recall the nausea she felt at meeting him. He was angry that he had ridden all the way to Dunstan Castle just to be rejected. Her father had compensated the man for his travels but Laird Stewart said that he would be back again after the harvest season when she changed her mind. But that was never going to happen. Annella would gladly join a convent before ever marrying him.

She pulled her chemise over her head and picked up the green gown Berta had laid down on the bed. *If only I was a lad, I would ne'er have to marry if I dinna want to…*the thought made her smile.

Berta came up behind her to tighten the laces on the back of her dress. "Why do ye keep running up that wretched hillside anyways? It's steep and ye could get hurt."

"I enjoy riding my horse, that's all," she lied.

Berta came to her front, lowered her head and looked at her from beneath her eyelashes. She knew her reason for running off and knew it had nothing to do with riding.

Riding to the top of the hillside was Annella's favorite place to be alone. From the hilltop she could see the beautiful countryside beyond the rolling green hills and vast forest. On the hilltop she felt free.

Berta's voice brought her back to the present. "My lady, ye cannae keep running off every time a mon comes to ask fer yer hand. Ye are already nineteen and it's about time to be looking for a husband. Just take a look at your younger sister, Nessa, she found herself a fine mon. It may no' be the love match ye speak of but she will learn to love him overtime, just as ye will with yer husband."

"Berta, I am no' Nessa. Is it too much to ask for a marriage to be bound by love instead of obligation? What if the mon I am forced to marry is an awful mon and ne'er even loves me?"

"Ach, my lady, dreams are lovely but they are no' real. True love matches are rare and dinna come around verra often. Fer a lady, all ye can hope fer is a mon with a good name who can offer ye protection," she replied as she softly touched Annella's cheek.

"I dinna need protection, Berta, I have my horse and my bow. No' to mention that I can best any mon who challenges me."

"Aye, I ken ye can, lass. Ye have grown up so much, Annella. Yer mother would have been verra proud of ye. It's been hard on yer father all these years trying to raise two daughters alone. And he feels that ye would be better taken care of if ye had a husband."

"Aye, I suppose so."

"I ken so. Now ye get downstairs before yer father gets in one of his moods."

Annella nodded and walked down the stairs sulking. She didn't want whoever the potential husband was to think of her as an eager bride, just the opposite. So she took her time, slowly taking each step one at a time.

Rory knew that gathering supplies at Dunstan Castle would be beneficial. They were only able to carry enough food and supplies for several days at a time. The laird of Dunstan Castle, Laird Hamish MacCallum was a lifelong friend of his father's before Rory's father passed away two summers ago.

Rory sat at the head of the table in the great hall with Laird Hamish. The room was smaller than his back at Dunakin and less furnished. It was dim and the walls were bare. It became apparent to Rory that the MacCallum clan did not have much coin to buy such luxurious things.

"Laird MacCallum, another attack on Scottish soil is imminent. Messengers have reported all throughout the lowlands that English troops have been spotted burning villages and pillaging. William Wallace is planning a rebellion. He fights for our freedom. I have come to ask for men to join us and supplies for our journey."

"Call me Hamish, lad," he said and then looked to address his guard, Alastair, "Talk wit the men. If they choose to leave and fight I will give 'em my blessing."

"Aye, my Laird," Alastair replied.

"What of Wallace? I hear that he fights with common men. What of the other lairds and earls?" Hamish asked.

"Right now verra few join us. Longshanks claims he offers peace by giving them property in England if they will follow him, but he is full of lies and deceit. He has raised the taxes to support his war against France and e'en they are talking about joining the rebellion against him. Wallace will take any mon who is willing to fight for our freedom, and his numbers are growing."

"I will see what I can do," Hamish replied.

While discussing terms with Hamish, in the corner of his eye appeared the loveliest sight he had ever seen. A beautiful young lass he had not had the honor to meet.

She wore a long tight-fitted dark green dress that dragged on the floor behind her. Rory continued talking with his host while nonchalantly taking glances in her direction. Slowly, she started walking in their direction. Her long reddish-brown hair was loosely braided and a few locks of hair had rested over her shoulders. The ends curled and slightly cupped each side of her small breasts. His eyes traced down the shape of her body, over her curvy hips and slender legs all the way down to the small slippers peeking out from under the dress.

He nodded in her direction to Laird Hamish, acknowledging the bonny lass walking towards them. Hamish nodded in agreement and they both stood and walked over to greet her.

Annella sighed and continued her way towards the dais where her father was talking to Alastair and another man she did not recognize. The stranger glanced her way but did not seem to take notice of her. They must have been in very deep conversation, she assumed.

The man was definitely from the Highlands, she told herself. He had the same strong brogue accent that her father had. She was good at distinguishing Highlanders from lowlanders because when she went to the lowlands to visit her grandfather, she could hear in his accent that he had an English tone when he said certain words.

Looking at the man, even while sitting down she could tell that he was tall. His shoulders and neck were thick and wide. His hair was medium brown and went slightly past his shoulders. Her eyes were drawn to his dominant jaw line and then up to his eyes. They were as light blue as the sky in the early morning. He was strikingly handsome. He stood up and walked with her father to properly greet her.

As he stood, Annella took the opportunity to admire all of him. Towering over her, he looked like a Roman God. Every muscle appeared perfectly sculpted. She was correct in believing that he was a tall man. He stood about a foot over her head. The colors of his kilt were green and red and showed off his large calves. She could tell that under his white tunic his stomach muscles and chest would be solid and strong and his arms appeared just as powerful as the rest of him.

At least this one is good looking, she thought. She wondered what it would be like to be held in such big arms as his. The warmth and protection she would feel while he tightened his hold around her. *Where did that thought come from? I should no' be having these wanton thoughts, I am no' marrying him*, she scolded herself.

"Annella lass, this is Laird Rory MacKinnon, Chieftain of the MacKinnon clan at Dunakin Castle. I had known his father Laird Duncan since we were wee bairns. God rest his soul," her father said a little choked up when he mentioned his old friend.

"My father often spoke verra highly of ye, my Laird," he replied.

Her father smiled in acknowledgement. "This is my eldest daughter, Annella."

As Annella's father introduced her, Rory was taken aback in surprise. Hamish was not what one would call an attractive man by any means. He was a giant Highlander with a heavy red beard and protruding round belly. It was hard to believe that this beautiful petite lass standing in front of him was his daughter.

Hamish turned his attention to Annella and said, "Laird MacKinnon has come to ask for…"

Immediately Annella's heart dropped in her chest. She pleaded to herself, *Dinna say my hand, please dinna say my hand.*

" … men to join him and for supplies," her father continued. "They have traveled from the Isle of Skye on an important mission to Stirling."

"Good day, my lady. It is a pleasure to meet ye," Rory said as he slightly bowed his head.

Annella raised her brow in confusion. They never had any visitors other than those pursing her father's lands by asking for her hand in marriage. Trying to compose herself and control her breathing she simply responded by nodding her head in return.

"My Laird, there is food prepared for the nooning if ye and yer men will join us for a meal," Hamish offered, and placed his hand on his shoulder to direct him back towards the dais.

Rory could tell that Annella was fairly nervous as she lightly bit her bottom lip. Her lips were plush and soft pink. They were kissable lips. Rory wondered what they would taste like. Her large round eyes were a beautiful hazel color and she had a small trace of freckles on the bridge of her nose. He had bedded many women before but none of them stirred his groin the way she was doing.

As much as Rory wanted to lift her skirt and indulge in carnal pleasure, he had more important matters to attend. Besides, she was innocent and he did not have the right nor would he ever take what wasn't his.

During the meal, Annella sat next to her father and listened to the men re-tell the rumors they had heard about the English. Paying attention had become increasingly difficult as Rory, who sat adjacent to her, kept staring at her. Trying to focus on the conversation, she gathered that scouts had infiltrated an English camp and heard they were establishing a plan to attack at Stirling Castle.

Annella knew that for years the English tried quite harshly to rid Scotland of those whom did not pledge their allegiance to the English King Edward. They did so by imprisonment, hangings or at the end of their swords. Warriors had fought long and hard for Scotland's independence. They had already seen many victories but had lost equally as many.

"And after all we have already sacrificed; ye believe that the English may succeed?" Annella asked sounding slightly pretentious.

"It is quite possible, my lady. That is why it is important to gather men to support our cause. But surely such talk is of nay interest to ye my lady."

"And why would I no' be interested? I may no' ken much of politics and war strategies, my Laird, but I ken enough and would fight for the same causes as ye do, if only I were a lad," she defended herself.

Rory gave her a cross look which made Annella feel offended. She thought that he must be the type to not care for an opinion from a lass.

"Ye ken where my allegiance lies. I'd lay down my life for my countrymen and take wit me as many of those dammed Sassenachs as I could," Hamish vowed. "I may be old but I still have some fight in me yet. If it weren't for this blasted bad leg of mine, I would gladly join ye."

"Thank ye, but that is no' necessary, my Laird," Rory responded. "It will take a good week to get there if we ride hard. I am to meet with William Wallace before those bastard English are expected to arrive. Yer assistance will be greatly appreciated and ye will be rewarded for yer courtesy."

"I dinna seek a reward. My keep may no' be a large stronghold as others, but it is formidable and our crops are aplenty. Alastair will help ye train the men. He is a good mon and a well-trained warrior. I trust him wit me life."

Looking at his daughter, he smiled. "Annella, tell Berta to have rooms prepared for Laird MacKinnon and his men."

"Aye, Father."

Annella stood up and headed towards the stairs. As soon as her father had asked her to go have rooms prepared, Rory noticed that she jumped at the opportunity to leave. He was surprised to see that she wasn't taking the steps two at a time. Rory grinned in amusement.

At the top of the stairs, Annella ran into Berta who was standing on the top step peering down at the visitors.

"Oh my lady, he is a handsome mon. Did he come to ask for yer hand?" Berta asked with much enthusiasm.

"Nay, thank God. He and his men are here asking for supplies. They have been requested to go on a special mission by William Wallace himself. They are just passing through and I expect them to be gone in the next day or two, and the sooner the better. In the meantime, can you please have the guest rooms prepared and meet me in my room afterward to draw my bath?"

"Aye, my lady," Berta muttered and hurried off to get the guest rooms readied for Rory.

As Berta walked off, Annella decided to go to the store room to oversee the gathering of the supplies that were being donated to Wallace's campaign.

"Spitfire, that one is," Hamish said while his daughter walked away, "and stubborn as a boar."

Rory curled his lip. Somehow this intrigued him as he was always up for a challenge.

"It has been my experience that most lasses are, my laird."

"Aye. Be glad ye dinna have a daughter. I have been trying to find her a suitor but she is being most difficult."

"Perhaps, ye will find one soon. If ye would excuse me, my Laird, I must speak wit my men."

Rory's cousin Ewan was one of the men who had accompanied him to Dunstan. He was second in command of their army and Rory's most trusted friend. They had seen many battles together and could always depend on watching each other's backs.

"Ah my Laird, sit, have a dram of whiskey wit me," Ewan said already feeling the effects of the watered down liquor.

Rory strolled over and sat on the bench next to him. "Ewan, we will stay here for a few days to train these men. I have secured additional supplies for our journey. Soon cousin, verra soon we will be in the midst of battle once more. Wallace believes that this surprise attack will be a heavy blow to those heathens and soon secure our freedom once and for all."

"Aye, my Laird. The men are ready to fight wit ye and Wallace. The stable boy has given our horses extra feed to ensure their strength for the long ride ahead."

"Good, see to the men. I am heading up to my chamber. We will meet ye in the courtyard after we break our fast."

Much later, Berta opened the door to Annella's chamber. Annella was sitting on the edge of her bed watching Berta as she pulled a large wooden tub across the floor and placed it into the center of the room. Bucket by bucket she began to fill the tub from a cauldron that was heating the water over the fire. All the while, Annella could not stop her wanton thoughts. The image of those mysterious blue eyes and the way he looked at her would not leave her mind.

"Yer bath is ready, my lady. I will be back after yer bath to help get ye ready for bed."

"Thank ye, Berta."

Rory swigged the last bit of whiskey from his flask and headed in the direction of the stairs. Those lips, they were all he could think about. He walked down the empty hallway in search of his quarters. He picked up a candle that was sitting on a small table and made his way down the quiet corridor.

The walls were draped in tapestries and portraits of the MacCallum clan. Rory felt the chill within the corridor from the poorly covered windows. Rory continued to walk until he got to the end of the hall; he stopped at a door after hearing the sound of someone singing. It was a beautiful melody and the woman's voice was enchanting. It had reminded him of a song his mother used to sing to him as a lad. As if hypnotized by the song, he slightly opened the door to peek inside.

And there *she* was, her naked backside facing him. Rory could see the droplets of water from her wet hair slowly descending down the small curve of her back. The glow of the candle light shimmered on her skin making it appear soft and creamy. Her round arse was firm and plump and Rory felt his manhood stiffen beneath his kilt. He wanted nothing more than to run across the room, toss her onto the bed and kiss every inch of her delicate skin.

While taking her bath, Annella heard footsteps outside her door. Assuming that they were Berta's, she began to stand up and greet the woman. However instead of an auld, plump woman, a blushing Rory stood in the door frame staring at the back side of her naked body. As the door crept open further, his massive size filled the expanse of the door frame.

"What are ye doing? Get out," she yelled as she quickly dove back into the water. She could feel her face burning bright red from both anger and embarrassment.

"My apologies, my lady. I was lost and unable to find my room."

Feeling embarrassed with himself, he abruptly turned around offering her what little dignity she had left. As he turned around, he saw two maids standing just outside the door. Annella's eyes widened like a scared deer.

"Good night, my lady," Rory said and swiftly walked past the two women and out the door.

"Oh my lady, what were ye thinking? Ye can no' have a mon in here wit ye. It's no' proper for a young maiden," Berta asserted.

"I dinna. He walked in here."

"That mad brute! Yer father would have him hung and quartered if he thought ye were bedding."

"Nothing happened, he said he was lost."

Myra, the younger maid with golden hair spoke up, "I will show him the way to his chamber." And with that, she walked out and ran after him.

Berta helped Annella dry her hair by the fire and put her nightgown on. She got into the bed feeling a little bit jealous of Myra. The maid was a pretty lass and often gave herself to the visiting men. Would Rory take her? She argued with herself about why she should care, but in truth she did.

All Annella wanted at that moment was to sleep the rest of the time away while Rory was here, hoping she could avoid him for that long. Lying in her bed, she could not stop wondering what was transpiring a few doors down. She didn't know what kind of man Rory was; whether he was one who slept with any willing whore or not.

"My Laird, I can show ye to yer room. My name is Myra. I can also give ye some company tonight, if ye wish?" she said with a sultry look of seduction.

Rory was intrigued by this promiscuous blond harlot who was willingly giving herself to him. It had been a long while since he had bedded down with a lass but, with all his traveling, he had no time for coupling. At first he was going to accept her offer, but after thinking about the episode in Annella's room, he was no longer in the mood. "Nay, I prefer to be alone. Thank ye."

Feeling irate by the rejection, Myra stormed off. It was rare that men turned her down.

Rory went into his chamber and barred the door. In a different circumstance, he would have taken the lass but he did not want her. He wanted someone else; someone with bright hazel eyes and luscious lips.

He unraveled his kilt and sat on the edge of the bed to unlace his boots. It had been days since he had a warm bed to sleep on. Camping out on the cold, hard ground was not something he personally enjoyed. He kicked his boots off and laid down on the bed. Staring up at the ceiling, the image of Annella's naked form was etched in his mind. She was like a siren that had somehow bewitched him.

He knew that tonight was going to be a very long night.

Chapter 2

Dawn came too quickly for Rory. He had tossed and turned most of the night. Still feeling weary, he thought the best way to wake himself was to take a quick swim in the cold loch. He hoped the coolness of the water would also help him concentrate on the day ahead and rid his thoughts of Annella. He knew what he needed to do was to ignore her while he was here. She would only be a distraction and right now that was the last thing he needed.

He had a mission and would not let anything take him away from that. He was a warrior and had no time for women and settling down with one was last thing he wanted. He knew as Laird he would one day need an heir but right now he had no plans to marry.

Several other clans had already offered their daughters to him, but he wanted someone who he could enjoy their company and not just the bedding. Someone who sparked his interest, someone like Annella, but he had to get that out of his head. In two or three days' time he would be off for war and he did not want to leave anyone behind to mourn for him if he did not make it home. His duty was to his country and his clan. If he shall meet the Lord during battle, his younger brother Bram would be next in line.

Knowing the morning was passing by, he tossed the covers aside and donned his tunic and kilt. He left his room and walked down the stairs. It was still too early to break his fast and most of his men were still asleep on the floor in the great hall.

Not wanting to wake anyone up just yet, he quietly strode out the door into the lower bailey. The way to the loch was along the backside of the keep and down the hill a short distance away. When he got there, he took off his clothes and set them along the shoreline and jumped into the water. It was cold but refreshing.

The sun had not quite ascended over the horizon when Annella awoke. She had wanted to get up early to take her horse Finlay out for the usual run. That however wasn't her only reason. She knew Rory and the men would be training in the courtyard today and she wouldn't be able to pass through the gates without him seeing her. She gritted her teeth thinking about the embarrassment she felt from last night.

She quickly got out of bed and put her riding gown on. Peeking out the door, she checked to make sure that no one was around. She frowned when she remembered that Myra had run after Rory last night. Feeling annoyed all over again, she grabbed her cloak and with stealth movement, she ran down the stairs and into the kitchen to sneak out the back door.

As soon as she closed the door behind her, she stopped to release the deep breath of air she held onto while trying to not make any noise. She took one step down from off the stoop, tripping on the length of her gown and landed in the dirt. Annella popped her head up to see if anyone had witnessed her clumsiness. Quickly, she got up to assess the damage. She had scratched her elbow from the fall and her hands were covered in dirt.

Annella scurried down the hill towards the loch to wash the dirt off her hands. She was just about to bend down to place her hands into the cold water when a figure suddenly emerged. Startled, she quickly ran behind a tree. She waited a moment to see if she had been discovered but heard no sound.

She turned around and sneaked a quick peek from behind the tree trunk. It was him. She knew that she should not be looking, but she couldn't get her body to listen to her demands. She had never seen a man before and now one was right before her eyes. Her breaths became heavy and she started to feel uneasiness in her stomach.

Rory slowly walked out of the water. Annella wanted to close her eyes but she couldn't draw her eyes from him. The corners of her mouth raised in the form of a smile when she noticed the water trickling down his flat stomach from the dark forested hair on his chest. She felt in awe as her eyes traced the lines and curves of his defined muscles. As her eyes went lower, she saw the dark curly hair around his groin which made her blush. And in a blink of an eye he fully surfaced out of the water.

Annella gasped at the sight of Rory's manhood. Long, hard and pointing directly towards her. Redness heated her face, but it was the heat she began to feel elsewhere that caused an unusual ache between her thighs. Her heartbeat grew faster. She feared her pounding chest was so loud, he heard her.

Turning around, she closed her eyes and rested the back of her head against the tree trunk. She didn't know what was happening to her and she didn't like it, mostly. She hoped that he would leave and that her presence was undetected.

"The water is all yers...my lady," Rory said standing directly in front of her with nothing but his kilt wrapped around his body. Stunned that she had been caught, she remained speechless and looked down at her feet hoping to turn invisible.

"I believe that now we are even, my lady. I have seen ye and ye have seen me," he continued.

"I was no' staring, if that is what ye were thinking. I walked down here and saw ye but a moment."

With a devilish smile he asked, "Did ye like what ye saw?"

"How dare ye ask me such a question," she barked pressing her lips together.

Staring at her pouting lips all Rory could do was think about how badly he wanted to kiss those plush, pink morsels. He took a step forward but she instantly retreated.

"Do ye always leave the keep unattended?"

"I have nay a need for guards. I can take care of myself and besides, I prefer to be alone and I have nay a need for yer company either."

"Do ye want me to leave then?"

With a mischievous smirk, he took another step closer and could feel her heavy breaths on his skin which made him shiver.

"I would assume ye have had enough company for one day," she snapped.

"What do ye mean?"

"I ken Myra went to yer room last night and I dinna pretend to ken how she is."

Rory looked into Annella's eyes and could almost feel the burning look she was giving him. He realized that Annella sounded jealous. But why, he wondered. He was going to enjoy this game.

"Ah, Myra, was that her name? Aye, she is full of companionship, isn't she?"

Annella's jaw dropped in shock by his remark and uncanny behavior. She had never met someone so callous and rude before.

"Ye are an arrogant brute," she said accusingly and began to walk away from him.

"My apologies, my lady."

Rory couldn't help his smirk. He found some humor in her anger.

Annella marched back to the keep and went directly into her room. The nerve of him, she said to herself, while yelling vulgarities in her head, directed at him. She aimlessly walked back and forth across her room not having the patience to sit down. She was too worked up. She wanted to go back downstairs and tell him what kind of an arse he was but then that would put her back in close proximity which she preferred to avoid.

A small part of her wouldn't have mind. As much as she hated to admit it, he was unbelievably handsome. When he stepped close to her, she was sure he was going to reach out and kiss her. She had never kissed a man before and the idea was both intimidating and intriguing.

Interrupting her verbal internal banter, she heard a commotion from out her window, momentarily preoccupying her thoughts. She walked over to the window and watched Rory and his men while they trained in the courtyard. The way he wielded his sword was quite impressive.

With only his kilt on, his upper body glistened in the sun as sweat rolled down his back and chest.

She observed him and his men for a few more minutes after realizing that she seemed cowardly by hiding in her room. Going out riding was the only thing that was going to clear her head. She grabbed her bow and headed out to the stables.

On her way down the hall, she passed Myra cleaning up one of the guest rooms.

"Good day, my lady. I trust that ye slept well last night," Myra said.

"Aye. Did ye enjoy yer evening with Laird MacKinnon?" Annella asked with an accusing tone.

"My lady, I dinna ken what ye mean. I offered my company but he dismissed me. Normally men invite me into their bedchamber but when he dinna, I left."

"Ye mean, ye dinna sleep with him?"

"Nay, my lady," Myra replied looking a little confused because Annella had never shown an interest in who she had bedded down with before.

That lying boar. "Thank ye, Myra."

Annella continued her way down the stairs, her head loaded with questions. Why would he lie? Did he purposely try to anger her? And why does it matter if he had slept with Myra or not? Feeling overwhelmed, she quickened her pace to the stables to saddle her horse. The sooner she got out of there the better.

The day was clear and beautiful, getting warmer with each passing hour. With her bow and arrows strapped to her back, she rode across the fields towards the loch on the other side of the forest. She needed to think, needed to be alone and needed to vent her anger.

She found a small knot on a tree and used it as a target. Notching an arrow onto the bowstring she took aim and released. Hearing the swooshing sound through the air, her arrow hit its mark. She scanned the trees looking for other potential targets and released several more arrows all hitting their marks as well.

"Ye are quite skilled, my lady."

Startled by the absence of noise, she turned around with an arrow still notched in place and pointed it directly at his heart. *How does he keep sneaking up on me?*

"Why are ye following me?" she demanded looking Rory straight in the eyes.

"Ye may want to lower that before ye accidently release yer weapon on me. For I do value my life, my lady."

Realizing that she still held up her bow in his direction, she slowly lowered it.

"I was no' following ye, my lady; I was already heading in this direction." He grabbed the reins of his horse and climbed down.

"Oh. Well then, dinna let me distract ye."
She turned back to her mark and released the arrow.

Wanting to stay and learn more about this
captivating lass he suggested, "I will make ye a
deal. If I hit yer next target I stay, if no' and I miss,
I will leave."

Wondering what game he was playing she
agreed, but only because she was not going to make
this easy on him. "Aye, I will agree to yer bet."

She looked up through the trees trying to
find a mark that she knew would be tricky to
achieve. Then she spotted it, a small knot on an Ash
tree several yards away. "There, if ye hit that knot
ye can stay, if no' ye must leave me alone."

"Agreed."

Rory looked over to where she was pointing
and grabbed the bow and arrow from her hand.
Placing the arrow above his thumb to keep it in
place, he carefully pulled back the string. Annella
smiled at his awkward body position and stance.
He glanced over at her and let it fly. Missed.

"Ha, ye missed," Annella said with a wide
grin on her face.

"Aye, perhaps I am no' as good with a bow
as I am wit my sword."

"That may be true, cause ye are terrible wit a
bow," she teased and burst into laughter causing
Rory to laugh as well.

For Annella it felt so good to laugh. It had felt like years since she had a good hearty laugh. With tears in her eyes, she smiled at Rory. When he smiled back, a sensation of warmth flushed over her body and her smile died quickly.

"Where did ye learn to shoot like that?"

"My mother, Mairi was her name. She died from fever when I was young."

"I am sorry to hear about yer mother. She must have been quite skilled for ye to inherit her talent."

"Aye she was. When I was young I used to watch her participate in target shooting with others in the clan. She would let me go out and practice wit her. After she passed, my father argued against it. He believed a lass should no' compete in a mon's sport. He is no' a verra understanding mon. He is a hard mon. But I ken if only he would give me a chance I would win. After all, it is in my blood."

Rory smiled down at her. This new insight into Annella's past made him all the more interested in wanting to learn more about her.

"Will ye be leaving now? That was our agreement."

Feeling disappointed for not coming up with another excuse to stay he replied, "As ye wish, my lady; I will have to practice the next time we meet. As soon as I find someone as good as ye to teach me."

"Maybe there is a solution for the both of us. I can teach ye how to shoot an arrow if ye teach me how to sword play," she proposed before she realized that she just invited him to stay.

"Sword play? That is quite dangerous, my lady, but yer suggestion has merit. It is sometimes good for a lass to ken how to protect herself and as ye so directly pointed out, I am no' as skilled with a bow. I shall give ye yer first lesson."

"Really?" Annella was unsure if he was serious or not but she had always wanted to learn how to wield a sword.

"Aye." He pulled out a long jeweled-studded dagger out of its sheath that hung from his belt. "Here take my dirk. Hold it in yer hand like this," he said demonstrating how to properly hold onto the hilt.

She listened attentively to him and mimicked his every move as she swung the dirk from side to side. With his sword he tried to block her advances. While going over each rule of combat, they taunted and teased each other like children at play.

"Verra good. Ye are a quick learner, my lady. Ye have already mastered the foot work."

She smiled up at him feeling good about her accomplishment and his appraisal.

"I want ye to keep this. You can use it to help ye practice."

"Nay, it is yer dagger."

"Aye, I want ye to have it."

Gazing into his fiery eyes, she could feel his intensity and emotion as he looked down at her. Feeling his unwarranted attention, she looked down at the dagger in her hands.

"Thank ye."

"My lady, I owe ye an apology for my behavior this morning by the loch and last eve."

Continuing to look down she softly asked, "Why did ye want me to think that ye slept wit Myra?"

"I dinna say I slept wit her. Ye assumed I did."

Knowing he was right, that she did assume made her feel foolish. She looked up and curiously asked, "Why dinna ye?"

"To be honest wit ye lass, I am no' interested...in her." He moved towards her so close he could smell the rose scent of her hair. She withdrew away from him in hesitation.

Not wanting to scare her off he asked, "Shall we continue our lesson?"

"Aye, my Laird" she said feeling nervous by his behavior.

"Please, call me Rory."

She nodded her head and he continued his lesson. They spent a good hour together going over the moves. Once he was confident that she understood the basic movements and tricks if an opponent attacked from the front, he wanted to show her a different tactic.

"Now if an opponent comes up from behind ye like this, ye will want to block his arm so that he dinna have an opportunity to take advantage of ye in this position," he said as he walked behind her and pressed the front of his body up against the curve of her back.

With one of his hands on her hip and the other holding onto her right shoulder she started to feel light-headed by the physical contact. Each breath became forceful as she felt his hot breath on the back of her neck. Both of them stood still. Feeling his thumb lightly rubbing back and forth on the top of her shoulder gave her goose bumps.

Feeling uncomfortable at the close contact, Annella leaped out of his hold, just as her feet got tangled up by the skirt of her dress. She began to lose balance when Rory scooped her up in his arms to prevent her from falling. Slowly, Annella pivoted and tilted her head up to him.

Rory took this as an invitation and brought his lips down to hers. It was only meant to be a light kiss but, when she began to kiss him back that was all the encouragement he needed. With his tongue, he pressed it onto her lips enticing her to open. When she complied, Rory swept his tongue into her mouth. Kissing her, tasting her. He threaded his fingers through the long locks of hair at the back of her head to deepen the kiss. With his other hand he placed it onto the small of her back and held her close to him.

Annella was not sure what to do, but took her direction from him and swept her tongue along his. He let out a deep moan and pressed her body closer and tighter to his. She lifted her arms and wrapped them around the back of his neck. She wanted more, but unsure of what more meant. Rory positioned himself between her thighs and she could feel the hardness of his manhood pressing up against her stomach. She found a sense of joy knowing that he was just as affected by this kiss as she was.

Rory knew he had to stop soon before he lost control. He could not take her maidenhood from her out here in the woods. He could not take it from her at all. But he yearned to touch her. He wanted her more than any woman he ever had. But he couldn't stop. His body would not cooperate. Her lips tasted like honey and he was buzzing like a bee.

Feeling the awkward tension between them, she abruptly stepped out of his embrace.

Nervously she said, "It's getting late, I must go."

Suddenly regret filled Annella's mind. *What have I done?*

Watching her stomp away towards her horse, Rory quickly ran over to her and grabbed her by the hand. "Please, dinna leave. Ye have nay any reason to fear me."

"I dinna fear ye. This should no' have happened and I can no' be around ye. Ye make me feel things, things I dinna want to feel."

Rory was not certain what she meant by that but knew that he too was starting to feel something for her as well. He enjoyed spending his time with her. He had never felt like this towards a lass before, but any feelings he had would have to be denied. He knew that he had nothing to offer her. No promises. No future.

He watched her as she picked up her skirt and set her foot into the stirrup of the saddle to mount her horse. With a jerk of her wrist she yanked onto the reins luring her horse Finlay into a fast sprint.

Chapter 3

Annella was the first to sit down at the table for the evening meal. Berta walked through the kitchen door with a plate of warm fresh bread in her hands. Looking awkwardly at Annella, she could tell that something was amiss.

"My lady, is everything alright?"

"Aye, and nay."

"I dinna understand, my lady. Ye are talking in circles."

"He kissed me," Annella said wondering if she looked as confused as she felt.

"Ach my lady, he kissed ye? When? Where?" Berta asked beaming with joy and dropped the plate onto the table.

"Aye. I dinna ken how I let it happen. It just did. One moment he was frustrating the wits out of me and the next I was kissing him," she explained as she tore a small chunk off her bread and popped it into her mouth.

"It's because ye like the mon. And why shouldnae ye? He is verra handsome," she smiled trying to convince Annella to agree.

"How can I like him when he makes me so…so frustrated?"

"Aye, ye have been saying that. That is how I ken ye like him."

"Why would I like a mon who frustrates me?"

"Because love my dear is a complicated matter, and it is no' every day that a mon makes ye feel this way."

"Love? Oh good heavens, Berta. Ye are getting daft in yer old age I think," Annella placed her hand over Berta's and smiled.

"Ye will see, my lady."

"Please dinna say anything to my father."

"I promise, my lady."

Berta turned to walk away just as Hamish and Rory entered the room with the rest of the men. Annella sat on the bench quietly not taking her eyes off the bread in front of her. She was nervous to look up at him. What would he think of her acting like she did? She wished she could take her meal up to her chamber and hide away the rest of the evening. She watched as the maids brought in hearty bowls of lamb and vegetable stew.

"Is this seat taken, my lady?" Rory asked.

Quietly Annella shook her head. She could feel her nerves tingle throughout her body as he sat down next to her. Leaning in to grab some bread, he brushed his knee against hers. Annella couldn't help glancing up at him. Looking into those soft blue eyes, she felt her chest tightened and breath quicken.

Turning his attention to Hamish, Rory said, "My Laird, I was grateful to have the privilege today to see Annella's skill in archery. She is quite talented. She is as skilled as my men. Ye must be verra proud."

"Ye did, did ye? She got her talent from her mother Mairi. Her mother was also quite skilled and just as beautiful. I only wish Annella would spend more time learning how to stitch and doing other proper duties or she will ne'er find herself a husband."

"Father," Annella said embarrassed by what her father revealed.

"Aye. Well, it is a lucky mon who can find a lass with a wide variety of skills, my Laird. One would ne'er be bored wit her."

Annella looked up at Rory surprised by his remark. She wasn't sure if it was a compliment or an insult.

"When will ye be off?" Hamish asked.

"We leave in the morning, my Laird. Tonight I will be camping out wit my men and we leave by first light."

Annella continued eating her stew in silence, all the while feeling a slight tightness in her chest. She felt saddened about Rory's dangerous mission. She was just starting to get to know him, not to mention that Berta was right. She did indeed like him. Feeling dizzy she asked to be excused and ran out to the stables to get some air. She felt so confused by how she felt.

"Good evening Finlay, my fair-haired warrior," Annella said as she brushed her hand along the coat of her young stallion. Finlay was Annella's best friend and companion. She leaned down to pick up the bucket of apples and held one out in the palm of her hand. Finlay eagerly accepted and took it whole into his mouth.

Annella looked into the stall next to Finlay's and saw Rory's horse stamping his feet into the ground.

"Do ye want one too?" she asked as she carried the bucket over to the stall door and held one out for him.

"Well go on. It's alright," she said extending her hand further.

He was hesitant to take it. He took one step closer and sniffed the apple then snatched it from her hand.

"Ye are going to make my horse soft, feeding him like that," Rory said standing in the doorway.

"Why is it that ye always startle me?"

"It is important for a warrior to have stealth precision, my lady. Ye are lucky, my lady, that Torran dinnae bite ye. Could have taken yer hand right off."

"I only gave him an apple. I think he was jealous that I gave Finlay one. Do ye no' feed Torran treats?"

"I do, but I have ne'er seen him take food out from the hands of others."

Annella looked down not realizing the danger she could have put herself in. Wanting to change the subject she asked, "Is there something I can do fer ye, my Laird?"

"Aye, I was wondering if ye would like to walk wit me. I have seen verra little of yer countryside and home and I wondered if ye would be so kind to join me."

Worried about being alone with him again she said, "I thank ye for asking, my Laird, but isnae rather late?

"The sun has no' set yet and there will be a full moon tonight providing enough light."

He started to leave when Annella stopped him. In truth, she did want to spend more time with him. She wanted to know if there was something more she felt for him other than attraction. Every time he came around, he made her heart beat faster and she could feel the blood heat within her veins. And a part of her wanted him to hold her and to kiss her again.

"Wait, perhaps if it were a short walk I can accompany ye."

Rory wanted to spend his last hours with Annella. He couldn't explain the way she affected him. He felt the tug of his heart when she stepped closer to him and the ache in his groin. He knew he could easily seduce her but he had to fight the urge.

"Shall we?" he asked as he held up his arm for her to hold as they walked.

"Aye. I would like to show ye something," Annella said as they began walking down the gravel road, past the village and up the hillside.

"This is quite a climb my lady."

"Aye, it is a wee bit rocky."

Rory reached for her hand to help her up the side of the cliff. Once on the top of the hill, he followed her to the edge and they both sat side by side on a large boulder.

"I often come here to be alone."

Rory looked out over the landscape. At this height, he could see for miles. The fields below were lush and green, the mountains and sky reflected off the quiet still loch. The sunset was breathtaking.

"Why do ye come here alone, my lady?"

"To hide from my father. Before my twentieth year, my father is forcing me to marry. If I am no' married by then I will have to marry the repulsive Laird Stewart."

"Why dinna ye want to marry?"

"I do, it's just when I marry I want it to be fer love. No' for my dowry or for some contract."

"It is true, my lady, that most women do no' have the right to choose their own husbands. One is chosen fer her."

"Aye, well I dinna like the way things are. I should be able to choose my own husband. What of ye? Why are ye no' betrothed? Surely ye must have a contract with some other clan's daughter?"

"Nay. I am no' ready to marry, my lady. I have given my life to Scotland and will no' be leaving a widow behind. One day I ken as Laird I must fer I will need an heir."

"Do ye think things will ever change for Scotland?"

"I do hope so, my lady."

She looked over at him and accidently brushed her arm against his. Just by the light touch she felt the goose bumps crawling up her arm. She looked into his hungry eyes and sucked in a breath as he slowly leaned towards her. He stopped just before touching her lips. She felt his breath on her skin. She licked her lips and leaned into him pressing her soft wet lips to his.

Placing her hands at the back of his neck, she slid her hands down the length of his torso. He wrapped his arms around her waist and lifted her onto his lap. Wanting to taste her flesh, he kissed along the side of her neck, down her collar bone to the exposed top of her breasts. Annella moaned loudly from the sensation. She felt her body beginning to tremble. She held onto Rory tighter, wanting to feel her body pressed against his.

Rory looked up at her and pressed his palm to her cheek. "To be honest wit my lady, I want ye. Badly I do. But I ken I can no' have ye. I have nothing to offer ye and ye should only give yer maidenhood to yer husband. I leave in the morning and well…if something should happen."

"Aye. I ken," she said feeling the lump forming in the back of her throat.

She swallowed hard and held back her tears. She felt angry that he was leaving, but she was more angry with herself that she allowed herself to fall for someone who was unattainable.

"I should go. It's late," she said and pushed herself up off his lap.

"I hope to one day see ye again, my lady," Rory said as he reached out for her hand and placed a soft kiss onto the back of it.

Blushing by his remark and subtle gesture Annella replied, "As would I, my Laird."

Once Annella was completely out of sight and was confident she had made it back safely, Rory went back to the stables. Mounting his horse, he headed eastward several miles away towards the burn where his men were training. He had chosen this place to secure their location in case the English had scouts of their own in the area.

"Colin, how is the training coming along?" Rory asked his second leading commander.

"Good, my Laird. These are fierce men and ready for battle. Almost two dozen men eagerly joined our forces," Colin proudly replied.

"That is good to hear, Colin. We leave in the morn. All of the supplies have already been packed. We meet Wallace within five days."

"Aye, my Laird," Colin said and turned back to the men to continue the training.

Rory joined in on a few of the scrimmages to keep up his strength and endurance. Colin's observation of the men was quite accurate. Rory was impressed by their skill. He knew that before Hamish had injured his leg that he was a strong leader and that he trained his men hard. Without his leadership out on the training fields, they had depended on each other and their loyalty to continue the daily drills.

Alastair had also been helping Colin train the men; however he was staying behind to guard his Laird and castle.

"My Laird, these men are good and ready. They have been trained by the best and ye will no' be disappointed wit a one of them," Alastair said.

"Thank ye. I am grateful for all ye have done."

"I am going to head back to the keep now, my Laird unless ye need anything else of me."

"Nay that will be all, thank ye."

After a couple hours of sparring exercises, the moon was high in the sky before they finished. Rory watched as his men sat around the fire. Being a leader of men and a Laird was one thing, but he knew that these men not only needed leadership but needed to know that, while on the battlefield, all men are the same no matter their rank or station.

Despite Lairds who felt that keeping a distance from others earned respect from those who served him, Rory was different. He gladly gave his life for these men. That in its self, made his men loyal and trustworthy. He was their leader but also together they were Scots all fighting for the same reason, freedom.

Several men had left the camp to go out hunting for their meal. Leaning up against a tree, Rory watched as they passed around whiskey and told stories of lasses they bedded, and battles they fought.

"I got 'em, that filthy squealing devil," Angus roared carrying a dead wild boar over his massive shoulders. Angus, only seventeen in age was one of Rory's fiercest and brightest. Since he was a lad, he looked up to Rory and followed him everywhere he went, hoping one day to become his trusted squire. Since the day Rory honored him with that title, he had worked hard to become a valued member of the MacKinnon army.

"Well, get him on the spit, mon. I be hungrier than a wolf," cried Phillip, one of the other men.

Once their prize was cooked, Rory tore off a piece of meat from the bone and sat down over by the fire next to his cousin Ewan.

"Ye are quiet tonight, my Laird. Something on yer mind? A lass perhaps?" Ewan taunted.

"Hold yer tongue, cousin. Ye ken more than anyone that I will no' be settling down wit a lass. She is a maiden and no' a common whore so there will nay be any bedding nor asking for her hand."

"Ye will have to marry someday, my Laird. Ye need an heir and…"

Casting Ewan a glare that would even frighten the most fearless warrior, he growled, "Enough. We have had this conversation many times, cousin. I am leaving for battle soon and it may be my last. I will no' leave a wife behind."

Feeling angered and frustrated, he stood up and stalked his way over to his horse and pulled a plaid out of his satchel as well as a flask full of whiskey. Laying his plaid onto the chilly forest floor, he sat down looking up at the stars.

The effects of the whiskey kept Rory's mind scrambling. When his thoughts should be on his mission, Annella was the only thing on his mind. Aye his cousin was right, he needed a wife, but wasn't ready to take one yet. What did he have to offer her anyhow besides a widow's life?

He knew that he had no chivalry like a knight and he did not know fancy words to woo the lasses. He was more comfortable in battle than to be surrounded by ladies. He was a warrior, raised and bred as one, but he wanted Annella. He wanted to feel her in his arms again, to kiss her, to touch her. She was so sweet and delicate. He started to feel his blood igniting with heat and desire. *Damnation!* Rory snatched the corner of his plaid and wrapped it around himself. Rolling over onto the ground, he willed himself to sleep.

Chapter 4

"I am no' ready to get up," Annella grumbled to Berta as she rubbed her puffy eyes. She had cried herself to sleep, worried about the battle ahead and Rory's fate.

Berta drew open the curtains from the window letting in the light.

"Well ye better get going if ye are to meet Gavin in the barn this mornin' to count the supplies. He told me that ye were verra anxious to start taking on more responsibilities and no' better a day than today. Though I am no' sure how yer father feels about that but I am sure we will find out soon enough."

Annella crawled out of bed and with Berta's help, she slipped her gown on over her head. Bidding farewell, she ran down to the barn to start her busy day. She knew that keeping herself busy meant less time to think about the kiss that was haunting her so.

"Good morning to ye, my lady," Gavin called out.

"Good morning, Gavin. It is a beautiful day, isnae?"

"My, ye are chipper this morning. Ye must have slept well."

"Aye," Annella responded not wanting to tell Gavin why she could not erase the smile off her face. A good night's sleep was the last thing she felt.

"Well, I will have ye start in here by counting the barrels and stocks. Report back to me wit the numbers ye come up wit and I will check them wit my own."

"Verra well."

Annella thought that a duty like this would keep her distracted but it was no use. Occupied by her bewildering thoughts she had to recount the barrels of grain several times until she was confidently able to reconcile her numbers. Her mind kept wandering to Rory, if he had already left his camp for Stirling.

She thought that taking inventory of the supplies would be a mundane task, but not today. Throughout the entire morning she wanted to bellow out on top of the hills with the elation she felt. With Rory, there was passion and excitement, two things she had never felt before. Her stomach tumbled and her heart fluttered at the anticipation of seeing him again. She prayed that God would be so kind.

Knowing she was unable to keep her thoughts at bay, she decided to break when she saw her father walking across the courtyard heading towards the entrance to the great hall. She began to follow him inside.

"Good morning, Father," she said rather perky.

"Good morning," her father grumbled

"Can I ask ye a question?"

Her father grunted in reply.

"Do ye really think there will be an attack at Stirling?"

"Aye. I do. Those bastard Sassenachs will be there and Wallace will run them through. What's bothering ye, lass? Why ask such a question?"

"It's just so many men are going, and some may no' return."

"Some men, or are ye speaking of just one mon?"

Annella looked at her father, mortified. Did he know what had happened between her and Rory? She had not told anyone, unless he did. *Oh Dear God.* She felt herself begin to feel nervous and bit her lower lip.

"Now, dinna ye look at me that way like ye dinna ken what I am talking about. I see how he looks at ye and ye at him."

"I dinna ken what ye are talking about, Father. Nothing happened and nothing is going to happen. He is no' interested in marrying me anyhow."

"Aye, well if he asks for yer hand, I will accept. He is a good mon and a Laird. I have had enough of yer disobedience, lass. By this winter ye will be married to a mon of my choosing. Enough of this love nonsense."

Annella sat there listening and just nodded in agreement. What could she say? The one and only man who she ever considered marrying had left and took with him her heart, but she couldn't tell her father that, nor Rory.

"Forgive me, my Laird, but there are visitors asking for entrance at the gates," Logan, one of the guards informed.

"Visitors? I was no' aware of any visitors coming. Let them in, but search them for weapons."

"Aye, my Laird," Logan said as he ran out to greet the guests.

"Annella, this conversation is no' over."

"Aye, Father."

Annella and her father quietly waited for the visitors to be escorted into the great hall. Shortly after, Logan and a group of five mammoth-sized men entered through the tall wooden doors and stood before them. The colors of their plaids were unfamiliar to Annella. She noticed that the pleats of their kilts were not folded and wrapped around their waists the proper way. She thought it was odd since Scotsmen should know how to properly wear their kilts. She started to feel a strange tension as the men stood there in silence scanning the room.

"Good day, Laird MacCallum. May we speak in private?" the oldest man of the group asked.

As soon as Annella recognized his lowland accent, she felt her suspicion as the tiny hairs on her arms stood alert. Why would a clan from the lowlands travel this far?

"Whatever ye have to say ye might as well get on wit it," Hamish replied.

"Verra well. Reports have surfaced that ye have recently been offering assistance to known criminals."

"And who accuses me of such allegations?"

"Have ye or have ye nay offered assistance to the Scottish rebels?"

Annella looked over at her father in fear. She wanted to speak up and defend her father but as she was about to open her mouth, her father shook his head at her.

"Aye, I have, ye filthy traitorous bastards," he said in a deep gruff voice.

"As ye have admitted to these allegations then according to the laws of King Edward, ye actions are treason and punishable by death."

The man on the far side of the room drew out his sword from under his plaid and grabbed Logan from behind and slit his throat. Another man reached for his sword and pointed it towards her father's chest. It had happened so fast Annella froze in panic.

Her father yelled to her, "Run Annella, run."

"Get her," the leader hollered and one of his men began to chase after her.

She ran into her room and barred the door. She could hear the man's footsteps hastily walking down the hallway, slamming each door open in search of her. Annella ran to the window to call for help but as she was about to yell out, she lost her voice when she saw the violent scene below.

Thick black smoke filled the air. The crofts in the village were set ablaze. Dozens of men were fighting in the bailey and the woman and children were scrambling about looking for safety.

Annella jumped when she heard the crashing sound of her door. She turned to look and saw the blade of an axe splitting the door in two. She looked around the room for a place to hide but had nowhere to go. She ran to the table and slid the dagger that Rory had given her into the pockets of her skirt and grabbed her bow. Notching an arrow into place, she aimed it towards the door.

Three men clambered in through the hole they had created in the door. Annella released her arrow hitting one man in the shoulder but did not have enough time to notch another arrow before the other two men grabbed her. She was hit hard on the back of her head with an object. Blackness came and she dropped to the floor.

Rory woke up from the noise as a few of his men shuffled around the campsite. The sun had just risen and he was feeling famished. He sat up and rubbed the sleep from his eyes, stretching out his limbs after sleeping on the hard compacted earth.

"Ewan, after we break our fast, we will leave. I am expecting to reach Campbell's borders by nightfall," Rory called out.

"Aye, my Laird. I will have the camp packed up," Ewan replied.

"Verra good."

Rory looked up at the dark rolling clouds in the sky.

"Looks like we are going to be hit by a heavy storm, my Laird," Ewan said.

"Aye. All the better the earlier we leave."

Ewan passed him an oatcake and water from a flask in his sporran. Together they walked over to the spit where the roasted boar was still hanging and coals from last night's fire were still smoldering. After taking his first bite, Rory was interrupted by Angus shouting in the distance. He was riding hard towards them.

"What is that lad fussing about now?" Ewan asked.

"I dinna ken, I can no' hear him," Rory answered.

"My Laird! My Laird!" Angus hollered out.

He rode as fast as he could towards the men in the fields. He jumped down off his horse and ran over to the pit. "My Laird," he gasped.

"What Angus, Jesu?" Rory loudly cursed.

Angus stood there a moment to catch his breath. "It's Dunstan, they were attacked. I just came across a young lad who told me that their crofts had been destroyed."

Rory and Ewan jumped up from the ground and began racing to their horses. The rest of the men followed closely behind.

Rory's attention went straight to Annella. Was she harmed? Consumed with fear, he urged Torran to run faster. He knew nothing of the welfare of her people or the condition of the castle. Nor did he know who attacked or when.

Racing through the forest and up the hill, Rory could smell the smoke being carried by the wind. At the top of the hill, tragedy laid out before his eyes. The roofs of the crofts were still burning and the barns had been destroyed. Taking a steady trot down the hill, he saw many villagers covered in ash and soot, weeping and caring for the wounded as the men worked hard trying to put out the flames. Whoever did this knew exactly how to strike and when.

"I need a group of ye to help out here in the village," Rory called out to his men. "The rest of ye, to the keep."

Several of them volunteered to help contain the fires. Rory continued his way to the castle with Ewan and Angus. As they rode closer to the gate, Rory stopped when he heard the sound of rope slowly grinding back and forth overhead. He tilted his head up and raised his eyes. At the end of a long noose, Hamish's dead body dangled from the top of the curtain wall. Rory quickly looked away.

"Cut him down!" he roared.

Annella. With speed and vigor, Rory dismounted and rushed into the bailey towards the front door of the keep, passing the bloody mess of wounded men and bodies that lay upon the ground. The great hall was full of villagers and servants who were tending to the wounded inside. Part of the roof had been smashed in and the tables were destroyed.

Spotting Alastair in the corner of the room holding onto a dying man's hand he called out, "Alastair, what happened here? Where is Lady Annella?"

With tears of anger in his eyes he firmly said, "They took her."

Rory panicked and felt his blood boiling. "Ye need to tell me, what happened?"

Alastair watched the man he was holding close his eyes and drift away.

"Damn those bastards!" he bellowed out and hit the stone wall with his fist. Turning to face Rory, he continued, "The man ye see lying here was my brother."

"I am sorry, Alastair," Rory replied.

"Early this morning, my laird, a small band of warriors wearing Scottish colors came asking to speak with Laird MacCallum. They were stopped at the gates and their weapons removed, or so we thought. They were traitors who have pledged to Longshanks. Dozens of English soldiers were hiding along the edge of the forest. Once the traitors were let inside the gates, we were attacked. We ne'er had a chance."

"Who was the clan that led them?" Rory asked trying to calm his anger.

"Dinna ken. They wore unfamiliar colors. I am thinking that they tried to conceal their identity. We ne'er saw who led them. I was told that he had his men snatch Lady Annella. I may no' ken who the Scots were but the English mon introduced himself as the Earl of Lancaster.

Ewan walked into the room and turned to Rory. "The Earl of Lancaster? There are rumors that he is Longshank's nephew. He has been appointed as sheriff and has been raiding across all of Scotland, killing any mon who is rebelling against his king. He is a ruthless mon. Kills even the women and children."

Rory spoke in clipped tones, "Ewan, gather a small group of riders. The rest of the men can meet up with Wallace to tell him what has transpired here."

Clutching Alastair's hand, he pledged, "We are going after them and we will bring Lady Annella back.

Chapter 5

The pain in the back of Annella's head prevented her from being able to fully open her eyes. She felt herself curled up on the cold hard ground. Her body shivered, reflexively trying to keep warm. She could hear muffled voices from somewhere outside but could not understand what they were saying. She tried desperately to remember what had happened and why her head was fiercely pounding.

Flashes of fuzzy images came to her mind. Keeping her eyes closed, she frantically tried to concentrate. The last thing she remembered was breaking her fast with her father. She was down in the great hall when…the *traitors*. Her eyes popped wide open.

She began to feel the panic shudder through her. She did not know what had happened to her father. The last thing she recalled was running up the stairs while being chased, leaving him behind to face the four other men encircled him.

She scanned the dark room and tried to figure out where she was. Her wrists burned and were bound together. The rope was biting into her flesh. After slight investigation, she realized that she was inside a large canopied tent. She looked around trying to find any means of escape but she only saw the one opening. Her stomach tightened with nausea when she thought back on all that had occurred.

Next to her sat a platter of moldy cheese and bread that appeared to be at least a day or two old. Consumed with fear and anxiety, she leaned over and emptied the contents of her stomach. She had never been so scared. She prayed that her father was well, that her people were well.

Assessing the damage done to her wrists, she assumed that at least two or three days had passed. She struggled to move and sit up but her body was too sore. She had not eaten in days and her muscles felt as if they had taken a good beating.

"Aw, the bitch is finally awake," a tall Englishman with black hair said to his comrade as they entered the tent.

The other man with dusty blond hair replied, "Yeah and she made a mess of herself." He gave her a disgusted look. "The Earl will be pleased you are awake, little wench."

Annella stared at them like an injured animal and did not say a word. Taking out his sword, the tall man walked towards her. Using the tip of his sword, he cut the strap of her dress so that it no longer covered her shoulder. Annella tried to scurry away and both men burst into laughter.

"Pitiful thing, aren't you?"

"What are you doing in my tent?" Yelled a husky man with peppered grey hair.

"The bitch is awake. Russell and I came to check on her," the tall man said.

"Well as you can see, she is awake and still tied up, now get out so I may have a word with my prisoner," the husky man replied emphasizing the word *my*. He watched the other two men leave the tent and sat down on a cot located on the other side of the tent.

"Who, who are ye?" she nervously asked.

"I am the Earl and Sherriff of Lancaster and I hope you do not have any ideas of escaping, my pretty one. If you cross me, I swear you will be punished before I get you back to Dumfries to be tried for your crimes."

"And what crime would that be?" she defiantly questioned.

"Treason. We saw the group of barbarians enter your keep and we know that they support your Scottish rebellion. Any man, woman or child who does not give their pledge to King Edward will do so or die. And I, my lady get to be the fortunate one who serves out these punishments as I see fit. Perhaps I should share you with my men or take you myself as my reward for my loyal services to the king."

Bile rose in her throat. Her chest tightened and she felt as if she was unable to breathe. She sat up with all her strength and replied, "I will ne'er pledge to yer savage king."

The Earl got up from the cot and walked over to her. He kneeled down and slapped her across her face with the back of his hand, making her fall back down to the floor. She raised her tied hands to her cheek feeling the burn from his slap and tears spilling down her face.

"You say that now, my dear, but you will learn your place just like your father. Know this Lady Annella of Dunstan; I am not known to be a man of leniency.

"What did ye do to my father, ye bastard?" Annella shouted.

The Earl snickered and walked out of the tent. Annella knew that her father had to be dead. If he truly was gone and most likely most of the villagers killed as well, who would come for her? *Rory.* Had he left for Stirling? Did he know what had befallen Dunstan? She had so many questions and no answers for any of them.

Annella held back her tears. Grieving would have to wait. She knew what she had to do now was gather her strength and attempt an escape herself. She couldn't depend on anyone to rescue her because she didn't know who would come for her, or if they even knew where to find her. No, she had to do this on her own. If only she had her bow she would pierce that man's chest with an arrow.

She rolled herself over to the plate of food and ripped off a chunk of the cheese that did not have mold on it. She also took a bite into the stale bread and forced herself to swallow it even though it tasted horrendous. She knew all she needed to do was to wait for the perfect time. After she finished off her ration of food she yelled out to the guard standing outside of the tent.

"I need some privacy please."

"I was instructed no' to let ye leave, my lady."

The guard was a Scot? Her eyebrows came together. Annella couldn't believe that her own countrymen would act so treacherously. Why was he here helping them?

"Surely ye can no' deny a lass some privacy. Please, I only need a moment."

"Fine but any tricks and the Earl will cut us both down."

The guard entered the tent and helped Annella to her feet. She was not able to stand without assistance as her muscles were from disuse. The plaid the guard wore looked familiar but Annella couldn't place where she had seen it before. It was different than the ones she had seen the men wearing who attacked the castle. He checked her bindings and once satisfied, he walked her outside to the nearest bush he could find.

It was dark outside and she noticed most of the men sleeping around the fire. She was surprised to see so few. She had expected an army. She knew that some of them would be in the woods on watch but with only a few behind to protect the Earl, they would be more vulnerable.

"I'll no' be releasing yer ropes, my lady, so do what ye need and be done wit it quickly."

"Ye are Scottish, why are ye in alliance wit the English?"

"That is no' yer concern. Now get on wit it."

It was nearly impossible to lift her skirt to relieve herself with her wrists bound together not to mention the humiliation of knowing she had an audience. But she did not want to complain or to struggle. Now was not the time. She looked through the trees towards freedom. If only her hands were not bound, she might have a chance. But with the guard holding onto the rope with a firm hand, it was hopeless.

"I'm finished," she said. The guard pulled onto the rope with force, jerking her and causing the ropes to dig more into her flesh. They walked in silence back to the entrance of the tent.

"What are ye doing?" A man shouted to the guard. His voice sounded familiar to her.

"She said she needed some privacy. I took her out by the bushes," the guard responded.

"Good. I want to talk wit the lass. I dinna want anyone to disturb me. Do ye understand?"

"Aye, my Laird."

Annella turned around and looked directly into the dark eyes of Laird Stewart. He forcefully grabbed onto her upper right arm and shoved her back into the tent.

"It was ye." She shook her head in disbelief. "Ye are the one behind all of this? It was ye who brought the English and attacked my castle and killed my father?" she cried out and tried to pull away.

"Hush now, my bonny lass. Ye dinna want me to get angry," Stewart whispered while pulling her tightly against him. Once he fastened the flap of the tent closed, he tossed her onto the cot.

"I dinna understand. Why?"

"Unlike yer foolish father, I gave my oath to Longshanks. In return, I got to keep my head and other benefits, I might add. The only reason ye are no' dead is because I convinced the Earl to no' kill ye. The only way to protect yerself is by marrying me."

"Nay, I will ne'er marry ye. I would rather die."

"Well, yer wish may be granted soon enough. But ye will marry me. Whether ye are dead or no' makes nay difference to me. I will still claim yer holding as yer widower."

Unlike the calm, but ill-mannered man she had met before, Laird Stewart showed his true self as brash, aggressive and downright sinister. She was thankful for not accepting his proposal when he first made an offer to her father. Fearful of what he might do, Annella yelled out for help but no one came to her aid. Laird Stewart quickly covered her mouth with his hand and with primal instinct, Annella bit down hard.

"Ye bitch!" he yelled and pulled his hand back. Once the pain went away, he raised it above his head and smacked her across her face causing her lip to bleed. He climbed on top of her, pinning her down with his weight. He squeezed her head between his bony hands and pressed his lips to hers forcing her mouth to open. He reached down over her breast and began to painfully crush it and caress the rest of her body.

She cried out and struggled underneath him but the weight of his body prevented her from getting away. She sent up a silent prayer to the heavens asking God to make him stop.

"What is the meaning of this?" The Earl roared as he entered the tent.

Stewart quickly jumped off Annella and waited for the wrath of the Earl to be unleashed upon him.

"My Laird, I was just convincing the lass that she should pledge her allegiance to ye and King Edward or face the consequences."

"Until her trial, no one is to speak to her, is that understood?"

"Aye, my Laird. However consider the matter of our betrothal. I had an agreement wit her father that we would be married in the spring. I was already offered her dowry," Stewart explained as he pulled out a piece of paper from his inside pocket.

"Nay. He is lying. We are no' betrothed!" Annella yelled and violently shook her head. The Earl ignored her pleas and looked at the document Stewart held out in his hands. Staring at the flap of the document, her stomach turned at the sight of her father's seal. *Nay, it can nay be. He wouldnae have.*

He replied to Stewart, "I see what you say is true. I shall grant your marriage to the lass. At Dumfries, she must stand before the court and pledge her allegiance to the King and afterwards the priest will give you your vows. She will be your responsibility. But know this, no traitor not even your little bride, will be able to save herself from the noose if there is any sign of treachery."

"Aye, my Laird, I understand. She will take her place by my side. Thank ye, my Laird."

Stewart shook his hand and together they left the tent leaving Annella alone.

Annella laid on the cot, curled up into a ball, crying. She thought about the letter Stewart presented to the Earl. What did it say? Her father could not have possibly made arrangements for her to marry him, could he? She had never felt more abused, humiliated, and alone in all her life. She didn't care whether she lived or died but she would not marry Laird Stewart and she would not pledge to Longshanks.

She had slept a few hours before she was awakened by the guard. "Time to leave, my lady," he said with compassion in his eyes.

He must have heard everything that had happened in the tent, she speculated. She sat up and allowed the guard to grasp her ropes and assist her to the horses. It was daylight outside and the light stung her eyes. The left side of her face felt puffy from the bruise Stewart left upon her cheek. She was helped onto Stewart's horse and the group of them headed south. Throughout the ride, Stewart held her waist and pressed her into his groin. Every time she tried to struggle, he held her tighter around the waist.

Chapter 6

Rain fell with intensity for the first few days of Rory's travel, making it difficult for both the men and the horses. He was fortunate that each night they were able to find shelter either in a cave or underneath the thick canopy of the dense forest. During the day the fog was thick and hard to navigate through, and the heavy wind caused the raindrops to sting his face.

"My Laird, they were here. I can see signs that they must have set up camp here for a night. The ashes in the pit are cold but still fresh. They must have left a day or two ago," Colin called over to Rory.

Damnation. He had missed them but knew he was on the right track. He worried for Annella's safety. He had no idea, no sign if she still lived. He only knew that his heart told him that she was alive. He couldn't explain it but knew she needed him and he was not about to let her down.

Rory had noticed several footprints in the dirt. At least two dozen were in the traveling party that held Annella. Rory had ridden with about a dozen men so the odds would be two to one. An easy victory for his warriors, he thought. Each Highlander could take on three at a time and not break a sweat.

"We should set up camp here. It's secure and away from the high road," Ewan suggested.

Rory looked at him with resentment in his eyes. Ewan knew that Rory wanted to press forward but he also knew the fatigue of the men and the horses. Rory realized he needed to make the decision with warrior's logic and not with his heart. Ewan saw it in his eyes that he cared for Annella, whether he wanted to admit it or not. It was not just guilt or duty that led him, it was love and Ewan was going to make damn sure that he opened up Rory's eyes.

"The men are tired and the horses need rest, my Laird," Ewan reminded him.

"Aye, ye are right, cousin. We shall have a short rest and then be on our way."

Rory walked away both annoyed and displeased. He would have ridden nonstop if he could, but he knew it would not be wise to make this journey on his own. He walked over to Torran to take him down to the river himself. He needed to be alone to think and devise a plan. His insides felt twisted. He felt helpless. Each passing moment was another moment Annella was in danger.

Sitting in the long grass, Rory plucked one blade of grass at a time out of the ground and tossed it to the side, angered and feeling that they were wasting time. He kept his attention fixed on his mission and duty. He began to think about the lessons his father had taught him about being a warrior. His father, Duncan MacKinnon, often spoke to him about honor, duty and the importance of not underestimating your opponent.

"Soon my son, ye will be Laird of this clan; and ye will face many challenges. Ones that I have faith ye will overcome. Ye have grown into a strong warrior, one who will lead this clan into greatness and I have pride in me to call ye my son."

As Rory sat on his father's bed, he had taken Rory's hand and placed it on the jeweled hilt of his sword as he spoke his final words.

Remembering the days that followed his father's death still made his chest feel tight with anguish. Rory looked down at his father's sword strapped to his belt.

"Am I interrupting?" Ewan asked as he sat in the grass besides Rory.

"Nay," Rory shook his head.

"Do ye remember when we were young lads and we would play in the woods pretending we were rescuing damsels in distress?" He smiled.

"Aye. I also remember ye always wanting to be the hero and made me yer servant," Rory softly laughed.

"Aye. I almost forgot about that part. But I always was the better-looking mon and the lasses always enjoy a mon with looks as fair as mine," Ewan said in return, being cocky.

"The lasses just swoon at the sight of ye. Must be yer plucky lips," Rory teased.

"Ye are such an arse."

"Is that how ye speak to yer Laird now?" Rory raised one eyebrow.

"On the contrary, only out of the company of others do I insult ye," Ewan laughed out loud.

In front of the men, Ewan would never dare call Rory by his Christian name, but when they were alone he never forgot that Rory was still his cousin and the same lad he used to play with, taking sticks and using them as swords to fight off invisible bandits.

Giving him a more serious look he continued, "Ye love her."

"What?"

"Lady Annella. Believe what ye will but the lass is real flesh and blood I tell ye and as bonny as they come. I'd take her meself if she was no' already *spoken* for."

Rory looked at him with a hint of jealousy. He did not want to think about Annella being with another man, especially not with his own cousin. "I do care for her, but love?"

"Aye, dinna be so foolish."

Rory didn't respond. Instead he thought about what his cousin had said. Is that what made him sweat every time he was near her? What made him purposely seek her out just to see her beautiful smile? Perhaps Ewan's assumption was right. Rory was starting to fall for her. He yearned to hold her again in his arms, to kiss her and claim her as his because…he loved her.

Ewan continued to look at him but said nothing. He could see the internal struggle Rory was having with himself. It made him happy to see that the thoughts inside his head were turning and hoped that he had somehow helped Rory realize that he did indeed love the lass.

"Let's go see how the men are doing wit the tents and food."

"Aye," Rory sat up from the grass and walked over to Torran to tie him up for the night.

With only enough food to barely sustain life, Annella's stomach growled with intensity. Her denial to marry Laird Stewart and her refusal to give the Earl her oath to Edward had cost her a good beating and a cold cell in the dungeon. She had no idea where she was and knew that no one was coming for her. Annella's hope was lost as she knew that her life would soon be cut short. Either she would be hung in the gallows tomorrow or the dirt-packed floor of her cell would become her deathbed.

The bruises on her face caused her pain when she would try to open her eyes and her throat was so parched that it burned when she would try to speak. She was stabbed with pain below her chest from where Stewart had aggressively kicked her after she refused him.

The dungeon had no light coming in and was cold and wet. Rain water had seeped into the walls and dampened the floor. She could hear the faint sound of mice scurrying about and droplets of water lightly tapping on the ground.

Her gown had been stripped off her body and only her ripped chemise remained. The thin fabric did not provide much warmth and she felt the coldness creeping in. She accepted her fate.

With her arms tightly wrapped around her body, she said a prayer that the angels would come for her this night. She spoke of all of the things she was thankful for and for the kindness and love she was given. In her mind, she was instantly brought back to the moment on the hillside when Rory had kissed her. Kissing Rory had been the greatest thing she had ever experienced.

With her eyes closed, she recalled how she felt in his arms. Her body tingled as a slight feeling of warmth crept down her spine. What she would give now to see him again, to tell him how she felt? To tell him that she did love him, wholeheartedly. She felt like such a fool.

"Pick her up. And this time dinna ruin her face," Stewart roared at the two guards outside the gates.

The two men entered through the cell door and lifted Annella into the air. Thrusting open the door to the outside, Annella's eyes were forced closed from the sting of the bright light. She had spent two days in the darkness. They carried her inside the large castle and up the stairs to the tower room. Stewart watched as she was tossed onto the bed.

"The priest will be here within the hour. A maid is here to help ye wash. If ye defy me again, lass, ye will get more than a good whipping," Stewart snarled and walked away barring the door behind him.

Annella lay on the bed, too sore to move. A young shy blond girl about sixteen years of age entered with an empty basin and a pitcher of water.

Quietly she held the water to her lips and Annella greedily accepted. She poured some water into the basin and dipped a cloth into the water. The maid gently dabbed the cloth onto Annella's face to wash off the dirt and blood.

"Thank ye," Annella whispered in a hoarse voice.

"Ye are welcome. My name is Caitlin. Ye really should no' anger Laird Stewart, my lady. He is a nasty mon."

"Where am I?"

"Ye are at Caerlaverock Castle near Dumfries," she answered.

Annella examined the girl and saw bruises along her arms. "Did he do that to ye?"

The young girl looked at her arms and pulled down the sleeves of her dress to cover them. Annella saw the shame in her eyes as she looked away. The two women remained quiet while Caitlin continued to wipe her down.

"My Laird, we should be past Campbell lands and be in Buchannan's territory now; we are no' too far from the lowlands. Should we be looking to set up camp?"

"Nay, we will ride a wee bit longer. I know of a monastery on Buchannan land where we can stop to replenish our supplies and rest the horses."

One of the monastery's residents, Father Gregory, used to minister at Dunakin Castle when Rory's father was alive. After his passing, the priest left to minister to another nearby clan before making his way to Buchannan. Father Gregory was like a second father to Rory and his brother Bram. More often than not, Rory was with him in the church serving out one of his many penances, due to his wild and disobedient nature as a young lad.

By the time they reached the monastery, the sun had already begun to set and the rain had finally ceased. He climbed down off Torran's saddle and gave the reins to Angus, who brought him to the creek with the rest of the horses.

Rory grabbed his bag and headed inside to greet Father Gregory. Buchannan Abbey was a small monastery. The thin slits for windows offered little light and did not provide much circulation to freshen the stale smell of the rooms. The floors were covered with old rushes and dust motes floated in the light of the chapel.

Father Gregory and the rest of the monks who inhabited the monastery lived off simple means. Eating only meager meals themselves, they offered whatever they could to fellow Scots in need. With the English burning villages and battles breaking out across the lowlands, many Scots were left helpless and homeless.

"Laird MacKinnon, it is good to see ye again, my young friend," Father Gregory said with an extended hand.

It had been some time since Rory had last seen him. The man now standing before him looked shorter. His hair had turned from grey to white and his beard was now a foot long. His robes were brown and matted, and his hands were showing signs of aging as well, no longer steady but shaky and bony.

"Father, it is good to see ye as well." Rory firmly shook his hand and offered him a brief embrace.

"Why have ye traveled so far? Last I heard ye were on yer way to join Wallace," Father Gregory mused.

"Aye, we stopped at Dunstan Castle for a few nights to gather more men. However there was an attack upon their lands and their Laird Hamish MacCallum has been killed. They took his daughter, Lady Annella, and we are going after them. It is my fault that this happened, Father, so it is only right for me to be the one to rescue her. Have ye heard any word on the English passing through?"

"Aye. Word has it that they passed through here several days ago heading to Dumfries. But it is no' just the Englishmen ye seek. The clan Stewart has joined them."

"Stewart?" Rory thought about the name for a moment then realized that Stewart was the name of the Laird Annella mentioned that her father was forcing her to marry.

Rory walked with him around the gardens that surrounded the monastery retelling him all that had happened. "We ask to stay the night, and then we must make our way when dawn breaks."

"Aye, of course. There are no' rooms for all of ye but plenty of dry hay in the stables to make enough pallets for yer lads."

"Thank ye. That will suffice."

"I hope ye dinna plan on doing anything foolish, lad. These be dangerous men."

"I ken. But I have to go."

Compassionately, he looked up at Rory with his grey eyes and smiled. "Ye just remember this; ye will face the darkness before ye are shown the light."

Rory nodded his acknowledgement and walked back to the stables. He found his horse and pulled out dry trews and a fresh *leine* from his satchel to change into. Taking out his plaid, he laid it down upon the dry hay to rest his sore muscles. Each time he closed his eyes, he saw Annella; her reddish brown hair and her remarkable large, round eyes. He knew rescuing Annella not going to be an easy task but she was worth it, in every way.

Sneaking into Dumfries when the English had already seized the castle was going to make this much more difficult. He would have to slip into the village undetected and keep his identity concealed to find out exactly which side the Laird of Dumfries was on; whether he was a traitor to his country or if he too was being held captive. Dumfries was a large trading community. Many people would be coming and going so he knew that getting in wouldn't be a challenge. The challenge would be getting out without being seen.

Rory prayed for Annella's safety and that no harm had come to her. He would not let Laird Stewart live if he had harmed Annella in any way.

With battle on the horizon, he realized he had a new reason to fight, a purpose. Over the past few days, Annella had become his flame in the darkness. He missed how her smile could brighten even the darkest of days. After meeting her, he no longer felt so alone. He realized that Annella was what had been missing in his life.

Chapter 7

Annella and Caitlin both turned their heads towards the door when they heard the sounds of multiple footsteps coming up the tower stairs.

"I am so sorry, my lady," Caitlin said as she held her hand.

Crashing the door open, Laird Stewart and the English priest entered the room.

"Nay, nay," Annella pleaded.

"Leave us," Stewart barked his order to Caitlin.

Caitlin gave Annella a look of pity as she hurried out the door.

"Lady Annella MacCallum of Dunstan, ye have been charged with treason for harboring known enemies of King Edward and for refusing to give your oath to England. Your punishment is death by way of the gallows. Prior to your hanging, we have agreed to your marriage to Laird Stewart so that he may rightfully inherit both your lands and your castle upon your death as agreed in the contract he possesses," the English priest said in a cold and heartless tone.

Stewart walked over to the bed and held Annella down while the priest mumbled in Latin, which Annella did not understand. She had assumed that he was either giving her last rites or reciting the vows of marriage. With all her strength, she struggled to get off the bed but Stewart kept her down with the strength of his arms.

"Do you, Lady Annella, take this man as your wedded husband?"

"Nay, ne'er!" she screamed and fought Stewart on the bed while he was beginning to remove his trews.

"Ye will be my wife, Annella. Ye have no choice." Stewart covered her mouth with his hand and bellowed out, "Aye she does and so do I, get on wit it."

"Then I pronounce you husband and wife."

Stewart leaned down on Annella and kissed her hard. Crying, she continued to buck underneath him. The priest stood watch to witness the consummation.

"Nay ye may no' have me, ye will ne'er have me!" Annella shouted and dug her fingernails into the side of Stewart's face drawing blood.

"Ye bitch." Stewart said and with as much force as he could muster slapped Annella unconscious.

The next morning Rory and Ewan looked down upon the village of Dumfries. Nothing appeared out of the ordinary. Rory saw merchants and traders busily hustling their goods and several villagers walking about. This was a good sign. Any sign of panic or threat would cause his plan to fail and he would not let it falter.

After a few moments of observing, the men rode their horses into the village below to uncover as much information they could about the occupying English. Rory and his men walked through the busy streets until they saw an inn at the end of the road. He knew that would be their best bet. Drunken men often had loose tongues. Rory and a few of his men entered the inn while the others went to take the horses to the stables. Once inside the inn they found a small round table near the back where they seated themselves, and listened to everything being discussed around them.

Not long after they arrived, a plump and fleshy woman came up to them. "Get ye fine men a drink?"

"Aye, whiskey," Ewan said back to her. Leaning over to Rory, he whispered, "Looks like nothing but Scots here. Do ye think we got here too late?"

"Nay. They are here, somewhere," Rory replied scanning the room.

The barmaid quickly came back with three mugs of whiskey. She leaned over to set them on the table, exposing her deep cleavage. With a smirk on his face, Rory asked, "What do ye ken of the English that came through here, my lady?"

"Seeking out the English are ye, my fine handsome mon? That will only get ye the end of a noose around here."

She gave him a devilish grin and placed her hand on his shoulder. Leaning in she pressed her lips against his ear.

"Rumor has it that now that Laird Maxwell has been away for a fortnight, they have detained Caerlaverock Castle until he returns. He has been charged with treason, they say. A group of riders just passed through here three nights ago."

"Was there a lass wit them?"

"A lass? If ye are looking for a lass, I can help ye with that," she said and gave him a wink.

"Nay thank ye, but I am looking for someone."

"Mmmph, Nay I dinna see a lass." She put her hands on her hips and snarled as she walked away.

"What did the wench say?" Ewan questioned.

"She said that the English are occupying Caerlaverock Castle. Laird Maxwell has been away and the English are charging him wit treason. They wait for his arrival. That must be where they took Annella." He slammed his fist on the table and swallowed back the rest of his whiskey.

Even thinking about Annella being in the hands of the English fueled the anger inside him with intensity. She had already been in their company for almost a full week and the fear and desire for vengeance inside him was escalating with each passing day. He needed to get to Laird Maxwell's holding and fast, while striking down every Sassenach he passed along the way.

"Sir. I do not mean to disturb you but the guards have caught a man lurking outside of the gates. He's a Scot and is demanding to see the Englishman who is in charge," an English guard informed the Earl.

"Is it that bastard Maxwell?"

"No, we do not believe so."

"Where is the prisoner now?"

"We have detained him in the upper bailey."

"Is he alone? Did you see anyone else with him?"

"No, Sir. We searched the area and found only him. He claims that he traveled here alone and is seeking out the woman we are holding captive."

The Earl had known the Scots to be full of treachery and was surprised that only one would dare come alone. This Scot must either be an idiot or just plain foolish. He sat up from his chair and strapped his sword to his side.

"Does Stewart know of this man? Perhaps he is kin."

"Stewart is in the great hall, I am unaware if he knows of the situation."

"I will get him and meet you in the bailey. Bring the girl."

"Yes sir," the guard said and walked out of the room and headed towards the tower to retrieve Annella.

Slamming the door against the stone wall, the guard yelled, "Get up." He pulled her arms to try to get her to stand but her knees buckled underneath her and she fell back down to the floor.

"Damn it," the guard murmured. "The Earl wants to see you, now." He called out to one of the other guards outside the door to help him drag her out of there.

Annella was unable to speak. With no strength or will to live, she had no choice but to allow the men to grab her from under her arms and haul her out the door. This was it, she thought. *Why God did ye no' take me in my sleep?* These men were off to take her to the gallows. She tried to cry out but no sound came out. Tears spilled down her face. She tried so hard to be brave but she had no will left; Stewart had taken everything from her.

The Earl walked down the passageway to the great hall and spotted Stewart drinking ale with his men.

"Stewart," the Earl hollered to get his attention. "We have company."

Laird Stewart set his drink down and stood up. He was uncertain who would have come but he enjoyed a good intrigue. The Earl explained the situation and both men walked out to the bailey together to see the Scot apprehended by the guards. The guards had removed his weapons and tied his hands together in front of him with ropes. He was down on his knees waiting for the Earl to present himself.

"Who are you and what do you want?" The Earl demanded and glared down at Rory.

Rory looked at the two men standing in front of him. The older man he assumed was the Earl of Lancaster and the other man he figured was the traitor Laird Stewart. "I am Laird MacKinnon of Dunakin and who are ye?"

"I am the Earl of Lancaster, personal sheriff of King Edward. I have been sent here to reprimand all those who support the Scottish rebellion against our king. Where do you stand, Scot?"

"My Laird, if I may, this is the mon who I saw enter Dunstan with his men. He follows and fights with Wallace; I am sure of it," Stewart whispered in his ear. The Earl nodded his head in acknowledgement, keeping his blazing eyes on Rory.

"I am no' here to discuss my loyalty. Where is the lass?" Rory's nose flared with anger.

"What concern is she to you? She has been wed off to Laird Stewart and has been tried for treason and crimes against our king. She is to be hanged." The Earl replied.

Married? Rory looked at Stewart, his eyes full of rage. His breathing was heavily labored and his muscles grew tense. Balling his fists together, he was about to jump up from where he knelt and kill the man standing before him with that smug look upon his face, until he noticed two guards from the corner of his eye. They rushed over, one on each side of Annella, dragging her by a hand under each of her arms and dropped her on the ground before the Earl.

She slowly lifted her head and felt her heart sink deep inside her chest. With a crackled voice, she tried to cry out "nay" as she saw Rory bound up and kneeling on the ground, held up by two guards. She shook her head, not wanting to believe that he had been caught. Knowing that he too, would die on the gallows made her heart break. *This is all my fault*, she told herself. *Oh Rory, I am so sorry.* She couldn't speak the words but the sadness in her eyes expressed the remorse and blame she felt.

Fueled with anger, Rory looked down at the dirt in front of him before he fixed his eyes back on Annella. Her hair was matted. The chemise she wore was torn and exposed much of her bare skin. Her bruised, tear-stained face made her almost unrecognizable. She looked fragile, like nothing remained but skin and bones.

His stomach churned. How could they have beaten this wee lass? What was once a fiery-spirited lass now appeared to be a scared, dying creature. He wanted so badly to cradle her in his arms, to let her know that he was there and would never leave her side again. With sympathy in his eyes he looked at her, willing her to sense his compassion; hoping she could draw some amount of strength from him.

The Earl looked between the two of them and said, "Is the whore really worth risking your own life? Is that why you are here? Do you honestly think you can save her?" The Earl laughed while his men joined in.

Rory did not take his eyes off of her. He said in a grim voice, "Aye. I would die for her."

Looking back at the Earl and Stewart, he had to hold his anger in. If he lashed out now, his plan would fail and he needed to get Annella out of here first.

"Good. Guards, prepare the gallows…for two," the Earl sneered and kicked dirt up into Rory's face.

The guards walked them both onto the wooden platform of the gallows while they began to string up the ropes. With all the commotion of the gallows being prepared in the bailey, the guards walking along the curtain wall of the castle had been distracted watching the scene below.

One of the guards standing by the tower began to retreat to his post when he was speared in the chest with an arrow. Quietly he fell without notice.

One by one the arrows flew overhead hitting the guards on top of the wall with precision. Hooks swung over the great wall and Rory's men began to climb. Once on top, they swiftly removed the bodies of the fallen men and cast them into the moat below.

Just as expected, Rory looked up and saw Ewan, Angus and Colin just above him with their swords in hand. He nodded and Ewan let out a blaring battle cry. The men jumped down from the wall ready to attack. Unprepared, the Earl's men scattered to find their weapons. Ewan cut down the guard standing over Rory and cut the bindings from his wrists and gave him his sword.

The sound of metal clashing, the smell of blood spilling and the sounds of men crying out in pain occupied Rory's thoughts as he held his ground. Trying not to fall or trip over the dead or wounded, he continued his assault.

Metal to metal, his men fought valiantly. One by one, they slashed Stewart's men and the English down. Rory looked around and saw many fallen men. Men with blades and arrows protruding out of their chests, ones with severed limbs, and men so young they looked to have never seen their eighteenth year.

Covered in blood, dirt and sweat, he called out to Ewan, "Stay here wit the men, I'll get Annella."

He came upon the two men guarding Annella. They did not have any weapons on them but a mere eating knife and a small dagger. They attempted to block Rory's advances but failed miserably as Rory slashed each man, one in the chest and the other in the arm. Rapidly, he picked Annella up into his arms and hurried toward the gates.

"Rory?" she whimpered.

"Hush now, I'm here. Nay more harm will come to ye."

With Ewan in front of him clearing his path, they ran back to one of the boats hidden in the brush just as Rory and Ewan had planned. He gently and quickly set Annella down, covering her in his plaid as they pushed the boat off into the moat toward dry land where the horses were tied up. He would have stayed and fought if circumstances had been different. He yearned for nothing more than to take down the Earl and Stewart but his first priority was to get Annella out of harm's way.

Soon Rory's men were trailing behind them. As fast as they could before the English caught up to them, they mounted their horses. Rory sat Annella on his horse and jumped up behind her. Lifting her onto his lap, he held her in his arms and raced off.

"My Laird, the bastards ran scared," Angus called out.

"What of the Earl and Stewart?" Rory asked.

"They're gone too; ran out as soon as we entered the gates."

"Damn. We'll get some distance between us in case they grow some balls and come after us," Ewan said.

"Aye," Rory replied.

He looked down at Annella. She appeared asleep with her head resting on his chest. Her skin felt feverish. He laid a kiss upon the top of her head and pulled her up closer to him hoping that the bumpy ride was not causing her further pain.

After a half day's ride, he found an opening in the trees with a nearby creek and decided to stop and make camp.

"Ewan, get me some water, bandages and salve for Lady Annella," he said as he slid off the back of his horse with Annella still in his arms. Gently laying her down on his plaid, he turned to her and said, "I need to look at ye, lass. I need to see yer cuts and bruises."

He unraveled the plaid from around her the best he could. When he moved her, she moaned in pain. His heart was breaking watching her in so much agony. He examined her injuries to see if there was anything that he could do but he did not know the trade of a healer. He was scared. Her fever was raging and he was not sure she was even going to make it through the night. The rope burns on her wrists were now blistered and her face and arms were covered in bruises. Ewan came back and handed him a flask of water.

"Drink this," he said as he held it up to her lips. She was barely able to take small sips.

"Here, my Laird. Ye can use my plaid as well for the lass," Angus offered sympathetically.

"Thank ye, Angus"

Rory took the plaid from his hand and wrapped it around Annella. Wrapping her in his arms, he planned to hold her the entire night if necessary to protect her. His men kept still and watched as Rory attended to her. They too felt bad for the lass.

"Ewan, I need ye to do me a favor. I dinna trust any other mon. I need ye to get to Dunakin as fast as ye can travel. I need ye to have my mother meet us at Dunstan. Annella's condition is no' good, and I believe that my mother's healing skills may be the only way to help."

"Aye, my Laird. I will leave at once."

"Thank ye, Ewan." Rory offered him an appreciative smile.

While the men set up tents and hunted for food, Rory gathered Annella in his arms and brought her inside one of the tents. Taking a wet cloth, he wiped her face down, trying to keep her cool and comfortable as she slept. He raked his hand through his hair and placed his head in his hands. He had never felt so helpless before. With tears in his eyes, he lifted up one of her hands and held it in his. He leaned forward and placed soft kisses on the back of her hand and whispered, "Dinna leave me, lass."

Chapter 8

Annella woke from a shot of pain searing through her chest. She looked around and saw Rory looking down at her and could see the tenderness in his eyes. She had been laying her head on his lap like a pillow. Knowing that this was completely inappropriate, she tried to move away.

"Nay dinna move. It will only hurt worse." He took his hand and placed it on the top of her head and gently glided his thumb across her forehead.

"Ye had me worried, lass. I was no' sure ye would make it through the night. I ken ye are in pain. I'm no' sure what I can do for ye out here. We dinna have a healer or maid here to help ye. We will ride back to Dunstan as quickly as we can. My mother will be there to help ye. She is a healer." He bent over and picked up a small jug. "I have brought ye some water to drink." He held the container up to her lips and urged her to drink. She tried to sip from the pitcher spilling some water down her chin. Rory used the sleeve of his *leine* and patted her face and neck dry.

She took a few more sips and looked away so that Rory could not see the tears rolling down her cheeks. She felt humiliated and angry. She did not want Rory to see her like this and she did not know how to tell him that Stewart forced her to marry him.

Making matters worse, she needed some private time and she knew that he was going to have to help her. For a man to help a woman to the privy was unheard of but she had to swallow her pride and ask for the assistance she needed.

With a shallow breath, she opened her mouth but nothing came out. Rory gave her a puzzled look.

"What is it, my lady?"

"I need some privacy," she faintly whispered through a throat gone raw.

"Ah." Rory looked around not sure what else to say. Normally a maid would help a lady in these matters but there was no one around. "I can help ye, my lady." He stood up from the makeshift pallet and as gently as he could he picked her up.

She coughed several times, moaned out and grabbed her chest. "I think my rib is broken. The coughing makes the pain worse." Even trying to speak was agony for her.

"We will have to bandage it up. It will feel better once we do."

They walked out of the tent to see the men breaking their fast.

"Good morning, my Laird. I have a plate of cheese and bread for ye and some warm broth for Lady Annella," Angus said.

"Thank ye, Angus. I am taking Lady
Annella out for some privacy. Make sure nay one of
ye leaves the camp."

"Aye, my Laird."

Rory carried her over to a small brook in his
arms and carefully sat her down on a rock. "I can
turn around if ye like but I will no' be leaving ye
here alone. I dinna ken this area and dinna want to
take any chances of someone coming upon ye."

Not wanting to argue because Rory did have
a sound point, she nodded to indicate she
understood and agreed. She slowly unraveled the
plaid from around her shoulders and tried to lift up
the skirt from her torn chemise but she was too sore.
"My Laird, I can no'…" she managed to choke out
in a strained whisper.

Rory turned around and saw her struggling.

"Here my lady, I will help ye but I promise I
will look away." He turned his head and felt for the
seam of the hem at the bottom of her skirt. He held
it up so that she could relieve herself.

Annella couldn't help thinking; *This has to
be the most embarrassing thing e'er.* "I am
finished," she said, feeling completely humiliated.

Rory dropped her skirt, picked up the plaid
from the ground, wrapped her up in it again lifting
her into his arms as he did so. As much as she felt
embarrassed by needing to depend on him like this,

she enjoyed being held by him. They walked back to the tent in silence.

"I will be back, my lady. I need to get ye some bandages for those ribs and I will get ye the broth that Angus made for ye."

"Thank ye, my Laird," she whispered faintly.

"Call me Rory, my lady."
He smiled. She felt her breaths quicken, not certain if it was because she was ill and injured or if it was her body's reaction to him.

Rory walked out of the tent and headed to his bag to pull out some bandages to wrap Annella's ribs. His body had been so tense while holding her in his arms that he had to make himself leave the tent to get some fresh air and relax. He wanted to take her pain away but at the same time wanted to ravish her.

Holding her in his arms throughout the night had been pure torture. Seeing her exposed neck and the flesh of the top of her chest made him grow hard with need. He had rubbed his hands up and down her silky arms in an effort to offer her comfort but it also gave him pleasure to touch her soft skin.

Thinking about what the Earl had said at the castle angered him. Was she really married to Stewart? Had Stewart forced himself on her and taken her maidenhood? He wanted to hurry back to Dunstan to leave Annella in his mother's care so that he could go after Stewart and kill the man.

"How is she, my Laird?" Angus asked interrupting Rory's thoughts.

"The lass might have a broken rib. I need to wrap it up. She is still coughing quite a bit. We need to leave as soon as we can. My mother will have herbs and potions prepared to help her heal."

"The men and I will tear down the camp at once, my Laird."

"Good, let me ken when ye are finished"

Rory walked over to the fire where Angus had set down the broth for Annella to drink. He took the plate of cheeses and bread for himself and the broth for her and headed back into the tent.

"My lady, I have brought ye something to eat. It is only broth but I don't think anything else would stay in yer stomach. Once we are back at Dunstan, my mother will help ye and let ye ken when ye can start eating solid food again. After we eat, I will wrap yer ribs. Then we must be off."

Part of her did not want to return, to see the damage the English and Stewart had done to her home. She wasn't ready to face the devastation that she knew would be waiting for her. Laird Stewart had taken so much from her. She made a vow to herself that she would have her revenge, whatever it took.

After only taking a small portion of broth, Annella felt nauseated and tired. Rory was glad that she appeared drowsy. If she could sleep while she rode on the horse with him, the journey would be much easier on her. He moved over to the pallet where she was resting. With the bandages in his hand, he gestured that it was time to examine her ribs.

"My lady, if I may I will look at yer ribs now. I need to see if they are indeed broken, and the location of the breaks in order to make sure that I secure the wrap properly."

Making sure that she wouldn't protest, he removed the plaid that was covering her. He looked up at her to watch her facial expressions to make sure that she was willingly to accept his help. He also wanted to watch for expressions of pain. Her eyes held no resistance and he continued to examine her. He placed his large hand onto the lower right quadrant of her abdomen and worked his fingers upward towards her ribs. With his hand on her body, he had to fight the urge to caress her. Touching her sent shivers down his spine. He felt like a brute, feeling such urge as he touched the wounded lass. But her skin felt so soft under his rough fingers, his body responded instinctively. Even bruised, she was beautiful.

Doing his best to suppress his body's response, he said, "I dinna believe these ribs are broken, my lady. Only bruised, but I will still need to wrap them. It will help wit the pain."

He unwound the bandage wrapped it tightly around the lower part of her chest several times tying it securely. As his hands came around the front of her to tie off the bandage, he grazed the underside of her breasts. The feathery touch of her mounds made him stir again. His mouth dropped and he looked up at her. He saw the reflection of his desire in her eyes.

She lightly bit her bottom lip and Rory felt his insides scramble. He raised his hand to stroke her cheek, not taking his eyes off hers. She closed her eyes in invitation at his touch. He started to lean in to brush his lips to hers when he was abruptly interrupted by Angus outside the tent calling for him. *Damn.* He let out a hasty breath and Annella instantly opened her eyes.

"My Laird," Angus called. "My apologies for the interruption. Ye said to tell ye as soon as the camp was packed up."

Staring into Rory's eyes, Annella read the same disappointment she felt.

"Alright, Angus. Ready the horses; we are leaving." Rory snapped. He stood and with one swift movement, he lifted her into his arms.

Annella felt an odd sense of coldness from him. She looked up and saw the bitterness in his eyes at having their tender moment interrupted. He lifted her up onto his horse and threw his leg up behind her not saying a word. She rested her back against his chest. Feeling tired, yet safe, she yawned and snuggled into the plaid Rory had wrapped around her. Before she knew it, she had fallen asleep.

Rory pressed Torran to run at a steady pace. Now that he knew that Annella had bruised ribs, he was concerned that riding would make the pain worse. He couldn't bear to cause her anymore pain. He held her close, hoping to ease some of the movement from the horse beneath her.

This action both calmed his nerves and made his blood burn hotter. With her arse bouncing up and down rubbing against his manhood, it took all he had to concentrate on something else and keep his body in check. *God in heaven.* He hoped that the plaid was thick enough between them that she could not feel the hardness bulging from underneath. He desperately tried to concentrate on the road ahead.

"My Laird, do ye think we can make it to Dunstan by nightfall?" Colin asked riding up next to him.

Quietly, not to wake Annella, he answered back, "Aye, we must ride as fast as we can but keep as steady a pace as we can. We can no' risk causing Lady Annella any further injuries."

"Has she said what has happened to her?"

"Nay and I dinna want to pressure her into telling me. I will wait until she is well enough to speak to try discussing it wit' her. I am no' sure she kens what to expect at Dunstan. She has no' mentioned her father, either, nor have I."

"The lass will be in for quite a shock, my Laird."

"Aye. I ken. My mother will be there to help her," he said looking down at the wee lass in his arms. *And so will I.*

He knew that losing his father had been hard on him and his brother. He couldn't imagine the blow it would be to Annella when she learned of her father's death. Damn Longshanks and his despicable, bastard nephew! He held onto the reins tighter until he felt the rope burn into the palm of his hand.

After a few hours of riding, Rory directed his men to stop and rest the horses. Annella was still resting in his arms.

"My lady. We have stopped for a break to stretch our limbs. Do ye need some privacy?" he whispered.

She looked up at him with blurry eyes and tiredly bobbed her head. Rory scooted back and swung his leg over to dismount. He lifted his arms up to take hold of Annella's waist and guided her down. Sliding her body down his, he held onto her

longer than he needed to. He put one of his arms
behind her legs and lifted her into the air. He didn't
want Annella to take the chance trying to walk, in
case her legs were still too weak, causing her to fall.

He walked over to some nearby bushes and
set her down on the slope of a small incline. With a
tree next to her, she raised her hand to prop herself
up as he adjusted her skirt making it easier for her
to lift it so she could relieve herself. Turning
around, he patiently waited for her to finish. Once
she indicated to him that she was done, he moved
around the tree to pick her back up and brought her
over to the fire where Angus was sitting. She
watched him walk away toward Colin.

"My lady," Angus said as he bowed his head
to her. "I have no' been properly introduced to ye.
Me name is Angus. I am Laird MacKinnon's
squire."

Annella coughed to clear her throat and with
a hoarse voice she replied, "Nice to meet ye,
Angus."

"I am glad that we found ye, my lady. Laird
MacKinnon was verra worried about ye. He cares
verra much for ye, I think."

Annella glanced over at Rory and inwardly
smiled. She too had begun to care a great deal for
him. Hearing someone else say it however, she
wondered if that was truly how he felt. At times she
believed that he cared for her but he hadn't said

anything so she couldn't be sure. But what did that matter now? She couldn't undo her marriage to Stewart. The vows were given by a priest and before the eyes of God.

Just then Rory sat down between them and handed her a small bowl. "My lady, I have some broth for ye and whiskey to drink to help ye relax for the rest of the journey. It will also help dull the pain. We should be crossing the border to yer lands soon and will be at Dunstan by nightfall."

The fear of what she would find at Dunstan grew stronger inside her. She kept telling herself that she needed to be brave. Now was not the time to cower. She knew that in her condition, she needed to get back home. Berta, if she were still alive, would help care for her as she always had. *Poor Berta, please God let her be alright.* The only good reasons she could think of for returning home were a hot bath, a warm meal and sleeping in her own bed.

Stewart's nerves jumped as the Earl forcefully swept his hand across the desk causing the stacks of maps and letters to go crashing down onto the floor. Still residing at Caerlaverock Castle, waiting for the return of Laird Maxwell, the Earl was angered by the loss of his prisoner and the attack on his men.

"My Laird, ye can put yer trust and faith in me. Let me take a group of men and ride out after them. I am a good tracker and my knowledge of the Highlands would come in verra useful to ye. I will see to it personally to kill that whoreson and bring my disobedient wife back," Stewart zealously offered.

Stewart was worried because he knew that the marriage between he and Annella was invalid as it had not yet been consummated. After striking Annella down, she had not awakened until Rory and his men arrived. He needed to have a priest witness the bedding or even the blood stained sheets in order to gain control of Dunstan lands and that was exactly what he was going to do.

Chapter 9

Before Annella knew it, they had crossed the border to her lands and were only a few miles away. The sun had already set but that did not stop Rory from riding.

The moon shone brightly offering enough light so that they could see the path ahead. At the top of the hill, they looked down over her village and Dunstan's keep. Annella froze. An eerie stillness hung over the village, and she knew that something was amiss. The village had been completely destroyed. Torran trotted slowly down the hill and into the village. They rode in silence observing the damaged crofts and barns. The village was vacant.

Annella's chest tightened with sadness. Were they all dead? She fought hard to hold back the tears and her throat constricted as she hid her face against Rory's chest. He tightened his hold around her. She needed him, his comfort, and his support.

The devastation to the village was worse than Rory thought. He couldn't imagine what was going on inside Annella's head. They continued to ride towards the keep. From a distance, he saw two guards keeping watch outside the gates.

"Halt. Ye there. That's far enough. Who are ye?" one called out.

"It is Laird MacKinnon. I have brought home Lady Annella."

"My lady?" The man called out almost in tears. He ran over to Rory's horse. "Oh my lady. We thought we lost ye to those devils. Thank God ye are alive!" The guard turned around and yelled out, "Open the gates, Lady Annella has returned."

The gates were lowered and immediately the guards in the bailey rushed over to them. Many of them praised God for her safe return.

Annella observed that the keep was also nearly destroyed. A part of the roof had collapsed and the rest was badly burned.

"It is good to see ye, my Laird. Thank ye for returning our lady to us," Alastair said as he stepped to the side of Rory's horse, holding up his hand to shake Rory's. Holding his arms out toward Annella, he said, "I can take her now. Yer cousin and mother have also just arrived."

"Good. Ask my mother to have a bath sent up to Lady Annella's room."

Seeing only a few of her clansmen, in a throaty whisper Annella asked despairingly, "Where is everyone?"

"Those who survived have taken refuge with the Dundas clan. Only a few of us remained behind, my lady," Alastair explained.

Rory put his hand on Annella's cheek and whispered, "Dinna worry, lass. I will come see how ye fair after my mother has looked over ye and ye have had yer bath. I promise." With tears in her eyes, she nodded her head and a guard gently carried her inside the keep. Looking back over to Alastair, Rory said, "I need to speak to ye at once."

Once she was in her room, with her eyes closed and head tilted back along the rim of the tub, Annella breathed in the warm steam rising off her steaming bath. The heated water had already begun to relax her sore muscles. She was home and nothing at that moment could make her feel any better. She gazed over to the hearth at the far end of the room and stared into the fire. She watched as the flames danced around each other. She could only wonder what her life was going to be like now, with her father gone.

She knew she would have to help rebuild the village, take account of their supplies, delegate the staff all new duties and so many other minuscule tasks she wasn't even aware of yet. Because she was now married to Laird Stewart, the land would become his, but she was not going to let him take it away from her. She thought perhaps she could get assistance from her sister's husband.

The Dundas clan so far, had been good allies. She knew she could count on her sister to convince her husband to help Annella organize the keep and perhaps offer her protection. She hadn't seen her sister for almost a year since she wed Laird Dundas. She missed her dearly.

Just breathe, she told herself. Now that she was home safe, her thoughts returned to Rory. Now that he had done his duty and returned her to her home, he would most likely be leaving. He had no reason to stay. As a Laird to his own clan, his people need him.

Thinking back over the past few days, she realized how strong her bond with Rory had become. He had helped care for her, fed her, and not once had he left her side until now. Now that she was in the care of his mother, he left to attend to other matters. Her heart fluttered in anticipation at the thought that he promised to visit after she bathed.

"Ye sweet thing. I can no' imagine why anyone would do something so terrible to such a young lass," Lady Kenna, Rory's mother said as she put her hand on Annella's cheek to assess the bruises.

Lady Kenna was a beautiful, kind woman. Rory shared her same dark blue eyes. She wore a long red satin dress and her hair was tightly braided. She was everything a lady should be. Strong minded, proper, and loving. It had been years since Annella lost her own mother and was enjoying the motherly contact she felt from Lady Kenna.

"I will help ye wash yer hair and get ye ready for bed. Ye also need to drink this. It may no' taste good but it will help yer fever and yer aches," she said as she handed over a cup of hot liquid. Annella took one sip of it and had to swallow hard to force herself to get it down. Lady Kenna was right, it tasted awful but Annella was not about to complain. Lady Kenna watched her as she began to lather up the soap in her hands.

Annella closed her eyes, feeling small tingles on her scalp as Lady Kenna massaged the soap into her long locks. When Berta washed her hair, she was much rougher. *Oh Berta.* She had forgotten to ask about her welfare. But deep inside, she knew. It was just another reason why she needed to seek out Laird Stewart and slice him with a dagger.

Once fully healed, she would get the full account from Alastair to find out every detail of what had happened. She just hoped that she could stomach it. Taking another sip of the hot liquid, her face cringed.

Once Lady Kenna had helped wrap Annella's ribs with clean bandages and put on a clean nightgown, she propped her up in bed and offered her some broth.

"I think maybe tomorrow ye can try some bread to help fill yer stomach. Tonight ye should rest. I can come back and check on ye later."

"Thank ye, my lady."

Lady Kenna smiled back at her and left the room.

Lying in her bed, she anxiously stared at the door expecting Rory to come knocking any moment, but after a long while all was silent. Feeling warm from the bath and covers, she began to relax for the first time in days. She decided to rest hey eyes just a bit while she waited for Rory to come.

Annella woke up to the sun shining on her face. After sleeping in the comfort of her own bed she felt well-rested.

"Ye are awake, my lady. Ye slept almost two days. I was worried about ye," Rory said feeling relieved. He was leaning back in the chair next to her bed. His hair looked tousled and unkempt.

"Are ye hungry? I brought up some cheese and bread. My mother said that ye should be able to eat solid food now."

"Thank ye."

She reached out for the bread and tore off a chunk and took the small pieces into her mouth.

"My Laird, I dinna get a chance to thank ye, for saving me."

"Ye dinna have to thank me, lass. I would have gone through hell and back to find ye," he said and looked down at his folded hands. Under normal circumstances, he would not have so easily spoken of his feelings.

"Which is why I must thank ye. Ye have brought me home and now that I am protected by my own people, I understand that ye will be leaving soon. Surely ye miss yer family and I can no' ask ye to stay any longer."

Saying the words hurt more than she expected. She did not want to see Rory leave but she couldn't ask him to stay either.

He rose from the chair and walked over to the edge of the bed sitting next to her. He lifted her hand and held it gently in his. He knew as Laird he had a clan that he was responsible for, but leaving Annella was not an option.

"My lady, ye are no' safe here and ye are still unwell. Most of the castle wall has been destroyed and in need of repairs and ye have lost many of yer fine warriors to the attack. With Dunstan only being held by a wee lass, a neighboring clan may see this as an opportunity to attack. Or…Laird Stewart may come to claim this land as yer rightful husband."

Annella looked down, feeling angered and ashamed of herself.

"My lady, may I ask ye…"

"Nay I dinna agree to the marriage and I dinna bed down wit him, if that is what ye were going to ask," she blurted out in anger.

"Then ye are no' married, my lady." Rory;s voice was quiet yet firm.

"Aye I am. The vows were spoken and before a mon of God."

"If ye dinna say aye and ye dinna lose your maidenhood to the bastard, then ye are no' married, my lady, and Stewart kens it. I think that is why he will want to come after ye," Rory said feeling grateful and relieved.

"I'm no' married, in truth?"

"Nay lass, ye are no' married. No', if ye dinna consummate the marriage. I will no' leave ye here to defend yer home alone. And I will no' be standing by and let ye be married to another mon."

Annella looked up at him in confusion. She bit her lower lip waiting for him to clarify what he meant.

"I will do everything I can to help ye and take care of yer people."

"But how? I dinna understand."

"Ye will have to marry me, lass. That is the only way to ensure yer protection and to cease the marriage wit Stewart."

"So it would be an arrangement of sorts?"

"Aye. I come from a powerful clan and can offer ye protection, my lady."

An arrangement wasn't exactly what Annella wanted but she knew that it would be the wisest decision. She felt foolish for thinking that Rory had any feelings of love towards her. She knew now that he was only being honorable by caring for her welfare. Feeling scorned, she bit back her pride and replied, "I thank ye fer yer offer, my Laird."

"No more harm will e'er come to ye again, Lady Annella. I will make sure of that."

"I ken," she said presenting a phony smile.

"If ye are feeling up to it, I can have my mother come in and help ye get dressed if ye would like to join us in the great hall this evening. There is much to discuss and of course we need to announce our upcoming nuptials."

"I would like that verra much."

"Then my lady, I will see ye downstairs." Rory gave her a small peck on her forehead and exited the room.

Annella sat back on her bed taking in deep breaths. *How foolish I am. Ye were right Father. Love 'tis a foolish dream*, Annella said quietly aloud to herself.

Shortly after Rory left, Lady Kenna came to help Annella get dressed.

"Ye are looking much better today, my lady."

"Thank ye. I am starting to feel better. The broth ye gave me yesterday worked wonders. My lady, I would like to wear my green dress and my black veil today. I plan to go down to the church and pray this afternoon for my father's soul."

"Of course, my dear. I will get them out of yer wardrobe," Lady Kenna said as she quickly went to the wardrobe as Annella requested.

Once Annella was dressed, Lady Kenna held up an arm to her to help her walk down the stairs. Annella's legs were still a little shaky but she was too stubborn to let them stop her. It had been weeks since she last visited the church and today was too important for her not to go.

The church was dark and cold when Annella entered. It had been abandoned for quite some time. The air was stale and dusty. The MacCallum clan had been without a priest for months. He had died from fever and the abbey had not sent them a replacement. She excused Lady Kenna and held onto the benches for support as she walked to the altar to light the tapered candles. She kneeled down on the dirt floor and made the sign of the cross.

Dear heavenly father. Forgive me my sins. Please watch o'er me and my people. I ask for the strength and courage to overcome what lies ahead of me. I ask for my father's soul to be wit ye in heaven and to be wit my mother. Please bless Laird Rory and all the people of Scotland. May we find our freedom from those who choose to do evil against us. Amen.

Annella stood up and walked toward the back of the church to the entrance of the cemetery. With pride and sorrow in her heart, she stepped forward and walked through the row of the freshly dug graves.

Chapter 10

Not wanting to disturb her, Rory quietly leaned against the door of the church. He had heard that she had gone outside without a guard and was unhappy that no one had attended her. With the English and Stewart on their trail, many dangers lingered outside the castle walls.

Annella knelt down in front of a large grave that he assumed was her father's. She had a solemn, peaceful look as he watched her arrange wildflowers near the headstone.

She wore a shade of green that matched the hue of the grass. The black veil covering her hair was draped over her shoulders and down the expanse of her back. She was the bonniest lass he had ever seen; it made Rory smile knowing that she was soon to be his. A part of him wanted to tell her how he felt but his pride held him back.

He shifted his weight against the doorframe causing it to creak. Glancing up in his direction, Annella gave him a soft sweet smile.

"I dinna ken ye were standing there," Annella quietly said as she stood up from the ground and brushed off the dirt from her dress.

"I dinna mean to surprise ye."

"There are twelve total, including my father's," she said looking down upon the graves.

She bent over and picked up a small stone and threw it as hard and as far as she could. "What matters of evil would cause a mon to be so cruel?" she said, infuriated.

She looked at Rory beseeching an answer, with misty eyes, wanting to make some sense of why it had happened.

"There are many evils in men, my lady. That is why we fight; to protect our homes and our families. My lady, why are ye out here alone? Ye should have a guard wit ye. I can no' protect ye if ye go out alone. It's no' safe."

"I dinna need a guard, I told ye that before. This is my home. I will no' cower away like a scared child."

"Ugh, woman. Are ye daft? There are English out there who have nay issues wit killing a lass. I am trying to keep ye safe, my lady," he said waving his hands in the air.

Annella looked at him with frustration and put her hands on her hips. She did not like being treated as a child. She understood his concern but did not appreciate that he underestimated her ability. She would not willingly go into hiding and let Rory fight her battles. Let the English come. She had hoped that even Laird Stewart would show his face so she could have the pleasure in killing the man herself…slowly.

"I will no' discuss this any further, my Laird," she said and walked past him back into the church.

"It's Rory." *Stubborn lass.*

Throughout the day, Annella kept herself busy to avoid Rory. She even tried to avoid eye contact with him from across the table in the great hall. Rory, Ewan, Colin and Alastair were sitting around the table discussing the further actions that needed to be taken to repair the castle. It would need to be completely rebuilt because in its current condition, it was not livable. They were speaking very cryptically and she had a hard time following what they were saying.

Annella watched as Lady Kenna entered the room with a jug of whiskey to fill their cups. Annella noticed that she looked nervous at first but when she looked over to Annella, she smiled. Wondering what was going on, she turned her attention back to the men.

"What did I miss?" Annella asked Rory.

Rory raised an eyebrow at her and gave her an inquisitive look.

"I can see it in yer eyes and the tone of yer voices. What are ye no' telling me? Please, I want to ken. I have a right to ken," Annella's voice was strained as she asked.

"There's nay use in no' telling the lass, my Laird. She will find out one way or another soon enough," Alastair replied.

"I dinna want to worry ye, lass. I was only trying to protect ye, as I said before. When Colin returned from the hunt this morning, he spotted a small band of riders heading in this direction. They are a wee day or two ride away," Rory explained.

"The English? Laird Stewart?" Annella quickly asked, looking back and forth between all three men. The tone of her voice became high pitched from anticipation.

"We are no' sure. It looks like they were wearing both colors."

"Now what? What do we do?" she asked hoping that they would stay and fight.

"We need to head back to Dunakin, my lady. We have more men there and will be more prepared if we are followed," Rory said as he stood up knowing that she was going to argue with his decision.

Quickly Alastair stood next to Rory. "My lady, ye must go with Laird MacKinnon. Ye are no' safe here. I love ye like me own daughter and I could no' stand it if ye were hurt or taken again. What few men are left, my lady, are simple farmers and only a small group of warriors. We can no' ask them to fight. Laird MacKinnon has offered those who are left a home at Dunakin as well as employment. Nothing is left for us here. Winter is coming and it will be too cold to start repairs. We have Laird MacKinnon's word that in the spring, we can return and build again. He also mentioned to us about yer upcoming marriage, my lady, and this union is what is giving hope to yer people."

Annella sat there and stared at Alastair. She was taken aback that Rory had made all of these decisions without her knowledge. Leaving, however, was one thing that she did not want to do. She did not want protection, she wanted revenge and going to Dunakin to be locked up in some chamber for protection by her soon-to-be husband was something she wasn't going to do quietly.

"Alright. We will leave, Alastair," Annella said with a flat expression on her face.

Rory looked over at Annella and could see the defiance in her eyes. He knew that she was angry with him but he needed to do what he must to protect his future bride.

"Tell the men to gather what supplies they can. We leave before sunrise."

Rory worried about only being a day's ride ahead of the oncoming danger but he hoped that they would secure sufficient enough distance between them to keep both Annella and his mother safe. He knew that traveling with two women would greatly decrease their speed but he trusted his men to protect the women with their lives. Rory turned towards Annella. Her lips were pursed and those eyes of hers were a darker shade of brown.

"Will ye meet me in the upstairs chamber, my lady?" he asked with a slight bow, motioning for her to precede him.

"Aye," she said and walked away towards the stairs.

Watching her walk away made Rory sigh. He thought it was cute the way she sauntered off, huffing and puffing. It made him smile. This wee hellcat of his excited him. Anxiously, he dashed up the stairs behind her.

"What is Dunakin like?" she inquired.

"Are ye worried ye will no' be happy there?"

"Nay, it's just besides visiting my grandfather's holding in the lowlands, I've ne'er travelled," she said giving him a sad look.

"I promise ye will like it. Dunakin is a massive structure, and can look quite intimidating to outsiders, but my mother has added a womanly touch to the inside making it feel like home. It is built high on a hill a short ways from the village. On the east side of the castle lays Loch Alsh. Many ships and vessels pass through the loch to reach the mainland but we dinna get visitors verra often as we have no port."

"I heard that the northern Highlands are beautiful."

"Aye, but no' as beautiful as ye."

Rory walked over and stood in front of Annella. He leaned down and planted a soft kiss upon her lips. Eager for his touch, Annella stood on her toes lifting herself closer to him pressing her lips harder to his. She parted her lips as did Rory, only this time it was Annella who bravely swept her tongue inside his mouth tasting his sweetness. Rory rubbed his hands along her sides feeling the curves of her waist and hips. Pressing his hips against hers, he grunted feeling the desire he had for her.

But Rory wanted to bed her properly. He wanted to be married first. Softly biting her lower lip, he slowly pulled away.

"Have my mother help ye pack yer things. I can send someone later to get what ye need that we can no' take on the horses. I will see ye in the morning."

Feeling hazy from the kiss that left her breathless, Annella smiled and nodded and turned in for the night.

After finishing off the last bite of his oatcake, Rory helped Annella onto her horse. Once the rest of the group was mounted, Rory jumped onto his saddle and grabbed the reins. Seeing that Annella was riding next to his mother with the protection of the other riders surrounding the tow of them, Rory took the lead and kicked Torran into a fast sprint.

Rory knew that in normal conditions it would take him two days ride to return to his lands, but traveling with women and especially with Annella still recovering from her injuries, they would have to add an extra day. Some of the terrain would be rough and he wasn't sure whether or not the women could sufficiently ride in the mountains. They would have to significantly slow their pace or he would have to find another route with a more stable path for the horses.

If anything happened to Annella, he would not forgive himself. He glanced over his shoulder to see how she fared and gave her a reassuring smile. She sat on her horse with such pride and proficiency. Her reddish hair loosened from its braid and fluttered around her head like wild fire.

Glimpsing over at Ewan who was riding at his left flank, he noticed a wide grin plastered on his face.

"What are ye so happy about?"

"Just waiting for ye to tell me that I told ye so." Ewan looked in Annella's direction and then back to Rory.

Looking at him with cold eyes, Rory replied, "Ye just wait until ye find a lass who tangles up yer thoughts and chains ye down to a marriage contract."

"Ha. There is no' a lass in all of Scotland who can tame me," Ewan said and raced his horse to pass Rory's.

Traveling deeper into the northern Highlands vast mountain ranges, the cool September wind blew through the valley. It was cooler than normal this time of year, and Rory became concerned with the fog that seemed to fall upon them. Riding in the fog made their travel much more difficult.

As they entered into the forest, the fog had become even more dense and blocked out the sun causing poor visibility. Slowing their pace, they cautiously moved their horses into a tighter formation and trotted through the mass of trees.

"I'm no' liking the looks of this," Colin called out.

"Aye. It feels as if there are eyes in these woods," Ewan agreed.

Rory adjusted himself on his saddle and placed his hand on the hilt of this sword. He too, did not like the look or feel of his surroundings. The Highlands were known to harbor thieves and highwaymen and with such little food and coin he carried, he couldn't risk their goods to be stolen by reivers.

"Stay close and guard the women," he said to his men. "Ewan, ye and I will ride ahead."

"Aye," his men answered back.

Rory pulled out his sword and carefully observed the sounds around him. It was quiet, too quiet. The wind had died and the leaves had stilled to an eerie silence. Looking around, he scanned the perimeter. Rory was about to give the all clear, just before he heard the sound of a twig breaking under a man's foot. *Someone's here.* He held up his fist to halt the riders.

"Men, spread out. Angus, stay here wit the women." He whispered so the uninvited guests would not be able to pinpoint their location.

"Please dinna go," Annella murmured to him uneasily.

"It will be fine, lass." Rory winked at her and looked at Angus, "Watch o'er them."

"Aye, my Laird."

As the men scattered, Annella watched Rory turn his horse around and trot into the thick fog. She swung her bow around and grabbed an arrow from the quiver strapped to her back and notched it in place. Moving her head from side to side, she readied herself for danger.

She took one glance over to Lady Kenna who was holding onto her reins so tight that she could see her knuckles turning white. She gave her a brief smile and drew her attention back towards the trees.

Please be safe, Rory. She sent up a few more prayers as she, Angus and Lady Kenna huddled their horses together. Angus moved his in front of them and held out his sword. For such a young lad, he was very brave, Annella thought. Angus had become a very good friend to her. He was always kind and helpful. It was apparent that one day he would become a great warrior and would help lead Rory's army. She was glad that he was here protecting her, but she wished Rory had stayed. She couldn't fathom the possibility of Rory getting hurt.

She wondered who these men hiding in the woods were. Could Stewart and his men have already caught up to them, or per chance just common highwaymen looking to steal loot from travelers? All she could hope for was the lesser of two evils.

Chapter 11

Without warning, an arrow brushed through Annella hair. *What the devil?* Turning around, she saw a long feather tipped arrow lodged deep in the tree directly behind her. She looked over to Lady Kenna as both women's eyes widened and their jaws dropped open in surprise.

"They are o'er here." Annella heard someone call out from a distance in the fog. She heard the sound of swords clanging together but could not see where they were coming from. It was as if the sound echoed off the surrounding trees. Squinting her eyes, she could see a figure approaching their small group. As the mass grew larger, she grasped that the man charging towards her was not part of their traveling party. He had his claymore held high above his head and was coming right for them. She pulled back her bow string and released her arrow, embedding it into the man's throat.

Angus looked over at her in shock, impressed by her skill and said, "Nicely done, my lady."

"I did nay intend to kill the mon. Just render him useless for ye to attack."

She had never killed a man before and was astonished that she didn't break down from the remorse. She had always wanted to be a wee warrior but had just proven herself a great adversary.

Notching another bow in place, she peeked over to Angus whose sword was held high as he gave her a reassuring grin. Looking around the fog anticipating another attack, she suddenly heard a loud thud and for a moment Annella's heart skipped a beat as her body instinctively shuddered. She turned her head towards the sound and locked onto Angus's eyes. The smile on his face slowly faded.

She saw his head drop down to look at his chest and her eyes followed. In disbelief, she saw the end of an arrow implanted in his chest. Angus instantly dropped his sword and slowly began to lean to the side. Annella threw her arms out to cling to his shirt to steady him on top of the horse.

"Annella, quickly, we have to get him down from his horse," Lady Kenna instructed.

Lady Kenna jumped down in between the horses allowing them to block any further danger and held her hands up to hold onto Angus' waist while Annella climbed down off her horse. Both women used all of their strength to help Angus down.

"Be careful," Annella said as she held his arms while Lady Kenna grabbed his legs and together, they slowly placed him down on the ground.

Looking at Lady Kenna she asked, "Is there anything ye can do?"

"I dinna ken. The arrow looks to be embedded in his heart."

She tore his *leine* away from the protruding arrow to examine his wound.

Quietly Lady Kenna lowered her head and said, "I...I'm afraid it is in God's hands. I can no' help this lad. Even if I tried to cauterize his wound, I believe there is damage to his heart."

With tears falling from her cheeks, Annella held his hand. His breaths became more and more unsteady. "It's ok, Angus. I'm here. Ye can no' die," Annella muttered and wiped the tears from her eyes with her sleeve.

"I...I...die w...wit honor, my lady," he stammered.

Annella knew that death was inevitable and that Highlanders' valued honor above all else. Wanting to acknowledge his bravery and valor, she sadly agreed, "Aye, Angus...wit honor."

Gazing deep into the young man's eyes, she saw the color fade. His eyes began to roll back and his hand went limp in hers.

"Nay, nay. Angus...Angus," Annella said shaking his upper body in attempt to wake him back up.

Never had she seen life taken from this world in this manner before. To see the soul leave the body while Angus was lying in her lap was an overpowering ordeal.

Lady Kenna came up from behind her and Annella buried her face inside her warm embrace. After a few moments, Annella heard the sound of rustling leaves and she bolted up and grabbed her bow pointing it in the direction of the commotion. Ewan and Colin came into view.

"Whoa, my lady. It is just us," Ewan said raising his hand guarding himself from her attack. "What's wrong?"

"Angus," she cried out.

They looked beyond the horses and saw Angus' body lying on the ground. Both men ran over to where he laid and kneeled down before him.

Looking around, Annella began to panic. "Where is Rory? Ewan, where is he?"

"I'm here, my lady," his voice came from a few yards away.

Annella turned around to see Rory a few feet away returning his sword to its sheath. She ran into his arms. *Thank God.* Rory stood back to look at her and saw her tear-stained face.

"It's alright, Love, I'm fine. We killed the bandits following us. They were no' the English and I dinna believe they were Stewart's men either. Probably just some local thieves trying to…"

Cutting him off in mid-sentence, she shook her head to correct him, "Nay, it's no' that. It's

Angus." She moved to the side clearing his view so that he could see everyone gathering over by the horses.

Rory ran over and saw Angus's dead body lying on the ground. He put his hand on Colin's shoulder and bowed his head. Colin had been good friends with Angus.

"We will have to bury the lad. We are still two days ride out and wit the English and Stewart trailing us, we can no' take him wit us. We will take his sword and his medallion to his father. And we will mark his grave." Rory's voice was low and full of sorrow over the loss of his squire.

The rest of the men gathered around to give their final goodbyes and blessings and walked away to find the materials needed to dig a grave.

The day was already getting late and Rory decided to set up camp a few yards away. Most of the men went out to hunt for their meal while the others quietly set up the tents. Annella could sense the mourning each of them felt. Angus had become a part of their family, this small band of warriors. Being the youngest, he was the most spirited and easiest one to poke fun at when the men would jest. But he was equal in size and his skill was well respected.

"My lady, the tent is set up for ye and my mother. I feel it is safer to have ye two together. We will have several guards on watch tonight," Rory said as he came to sit down next to her.

She could see it in his eyes, the regret he felt. She wanted nothing more than to be with him tonight and be held safe in his arms. But she knew that in addition to maintaining propriety, he needed to know that she and his mother were safe and agreed that it was the best idea.

"Aye, my Laird," Annella said as she got up and walked with Lady Kenna over to her tent to go to sleep.

"I ken that look in yer eyes, cousin," Ewan said as he sat next to Rory.

"Aye. I'm worried. We still have a lot of land to cover and our strength is now reduced by one," Rory said, fiddling and carving into the log he was sitting on with his dagger.

"We will get to Dunakin before the English or Laird Stewart reaches us. They will be foolish to attack us then wit our full army behind us. Dinna feel blame for Angus' death. He was a good mon and did his duty. I have been meaning to ask ye. If Wallace recruits again, I would like yer blessing to join him on my own. Ye will be married soon and have a clan to lead and Colin can manage helping ye lead the men. I am only a warrior. I have no' a home of my own or wife to leave behind."

Rory looked at him wanting to deny his request for his blessing but he knew that Ewan would go whether he liked it or not.

"Ewan, ye have a home. Always will. But aye, I would give ye yer blessing but only on one condition. After ye are done ye get yer ugly arse back home to us or yer mother and father would be the death of me for letting ye leave in the first place." Rory punched him in the arm and both men smiled in amusement.

"Here, drink yer whiskey, ye bastard," Ewan said jokingly as he thrust Rory's flask into his chest. "I will take first watch." Ewan stood up and walked over to the trees.

Knowing that tomorrow's ride would bring another challenging day, Rory decided to go into his tent and get some sleep. They would be riding through muddy bogs and rocky outcrops. Neither terrain was well-suited for horses but it would be the fastest route to take. He didn't believe that the English or Stewart would dare take their men through there and put their horses at risk. Rory was familiar with the area so he knew all of the secret twists and turns to take and which to avoid.

Lying on his plaid, he tossed and turned, struggling to ease the guilt he felt. His guilt wasn't only for feeling the blame of Angus' death but for how his lack of judgment could have caused Annella her life. Annella should never have been that close to danger. He felt he had been careless regardless of what Ewan said.

The next morning the rain set in making the ground even more muddy and uneven than usual. The horses struggled as Rory pushed them forward through the rocky terrain. Cold and wet, Annella wrapped her cloak tighter around her shoulders and kept her head down so the rain would not hit her face. She trusted Finlay to take his lead from the other horses without her having to direct him.

After hours of riding, her body started feeling the toll of the bad weather and the difficult terrain. Her thigh muscles ached from squeezing them tightly around Finlay's large midsection and her rump began to feel numb. But worst of all, she couldn't get the vision of Angus' eyes out of her mind. It was as if in the last moments of his life, she saw into his soul. She felt blessed being the one to comfort him as he drew his final breath before he left this mortal world.

Justice for Angus' death was meted out when Rory and his men slayed the outlaws in the woods. She felt pity that Angus' death was caused by nothing more than the greed of men looking for a small bounty to fill their coffers.

Slowing his pace down, Rory came to ride by her side.

"How are ye doing, my lady?"

"I am feeling a wee winded, my Laird. But please dinna stop on my behalf."

"Nay we should stop soon. A cavern is ahead where we can stop and build a fire to warm ourselves until the rain and drizzle passes. It's just on the other side of this pass," he said giving her a pleasant smile.

"Thank ye. That would be lovely."

Once they were around the bend, Annella saw the cavern Rory mentioned. It looked very inviting and well out of the rain. She looked forward to waiting out the storm in front of a nice warm fire and filling her grumbling belly.

Dismounting her horse with the others, she slipped inside and found a dry flat stone to sit on while the men went to gather dry wood for a fire.

"My lady, a large boulder is just over there. It may offer ye enough privacy if ye would like to get out of yer wet clothes and put on dry ones. The rain should be gone soon," Rory said as he pointed in the direction of the boulder.

"Thank ye, I would like that verra much." Anxious to get out of her wet dress, she scampered over to where she set down her belongings, pulled out clean garments and went behind the large rock. She slipped into a new riding dress. Putting on the dry dress made her feel so much better, inside and out.

Walking over to sit by the fire, she combed out her hair in an attempt to dry it as best she could. Filling the entryway of the cave stood Rory, glaring in her direction. She could smell the whiskey coming from him from across the room. She couldn't decide if he drank it or bathed in it.

"Would ye like something to eat, my lady?" Rory offered holding out some cheese and dried meat as he sat down next to her.

"Thank ye," she said holding her hand up to take the offering.

"My lady, I wanted to say to ye that I ken that ye have had a difficult time these last few weeks, and e'en though I am no' good at talking to lasses about these matters, I want ye to ken that ye can talk to me if ye are bothered or feeling...well ye ken what I mean," Rory struggled to say the right words, his head feeling clouded.

She put her hand on top of his and smiled. "Thank ye. But I am fine, truly. I will say that I was verra worried that something could have happened to ye back in the woods when we were attacked. Rory, before when I said that ye make me feel things that I dinna want to feel, well I..."

Before she could finish, Ewan jumped between them and excitedly declared, "My Laird, my lady, the rain has stopped and a few of the men just spotted what appear to be the men who have been following us along the ridge of the mountain. I

dinna believe they ken our whereabouts but I think
we should leave immediately."

Chapter 12

The Isle of Skye was just as beautiful as Annella dreamt it would be. The vibrant colors, the lovely smell of wildflowers, it was magical. The land was dominated by heather and fields of purple thistles. The rock outcrops jutted out of the ground as if they were strategically placed and the mountain tops touched the heavens.

Riding through the fields on the back of her horse, she saw off in the distance sheep grazing in the fields and could almost smell the salt of the ocean as they drew closer to the shore. With the fog and dark clouds gone, the sun shone brightly and Annella felt her spirit lift as the beams of light glistened off her hair and dress in hues of golds and reds.

After two days of rough riding they were finally climbing the last rise that looked down upon the MacKinnon land. Anxious to see Rory's vast dwelling below, Annella encouraged Finlay to ride faster. Passing Ewan and Rory she raced to the top of the hillside.

Looking down at the village and the dark castle in the distance made Annella tremble. The castle had a towering and overwhelming look about it, even from a distance. She swallowed hard. This was to be her new home when she married Rory.

Feeling her nervousness, she clasped the reins tighter and bit down on her lower lip.

Aware of her apprehension, Rory rode up next to her and reached out to hold her hand. She glanced over to him and saw his big smile. He was happy to be home. His smile comforted her.

"Come," he said and rode down the hill in front of her.

Entering the village, Annella watched as villagers cheered for the safe return of their Laird. Men, women, and even small children waved as they passed by. She was impressed watching Rory call out to so many of them by name. Annella gathered from the warm greetings that the MacKinnon clan were very welcoming people.

"Tonight we feast for the return of our Laird and his upcoming marriage to Lady Annella MacCallum," Ewan pronounced in a loud booming voice while the crowd applauded.

Before she turned her head back to the crowd, Annella felt all eyes upon her. Knowing that these people must be curious about her, she sat tall on her horse and bowed her head to them. She hoped that these people would come to accept her, an outsider.

In the corner of her eye, she saw an auld man and woman frantically scanning the men's faces as they rode their horses through the village.

Rory must have seen them too as he lowered his head, reluctant to look into their misty eyes.

Dismounting his horse, he walked over to Ewan who had also dismounted. Together with Angus' sword spread out across Rory's hands, they walked over to face the distressed-looking couple. At the sight of the sword, the woman collapsed into the man's arms weeping. The man took the sword with a loose grip and the tip of it fell and dug into the ground. "My boy," he cried out and held his wife.

Annella's eyes instantly filled with tears and her heart ached for them. Annella knew the couple was Angus' parents the moment she saw them. She felt sympathy for their loss and pain. She slipped off her horse and walked over to the grieving couple.

"He was a good mon and fought bravely. Ye should be proud of him." She heard Rory say to them as he placed his hand on the man's shoulder.

Annella bent down to Angus's mother and placed her hands over hers to console her.

"He was verra noble. I held him in my arms when he died. He spoke of bravery and honor. He saved my life and now my debt is owed to you, my lady."

The auld woman looked up with teary eyes and seemed to take comfort in her words. The man nodded and picked his wife up off her knees to help her stand. With his arm wrapped around her thin waist, they turned away from the crowd and walked towards one of the small crofts. The crowd of people became silent with grief. Annella looked up at Rory and saw the sadness in his eyes.

Looking among the crowd, she saw a handsome man that resembled Rory in size and stature standing far in the back. His big shoulders and broad chest stood out from the group of people clustered around the horses. His arms were crossed in front of his chest and he gave Rory a most disturbing glare.

Hand in hand, Rory and Annella walked over to him.

"So, I see ye go off to war and come back wit a lass. A prize? Or did ye steal yerself a bride?" the man said with an awkward expression on his face.

"Hello, Bram. It is good to see ye too," Rory said not letting go of Annella's hand. "I would like to introduce ye to the future Lady MacKinnon, Lady Annella MacCallum. My lady, this is my younger brother Bram."

"It is nice to meet ye," she hesitantly said as she felt his lusting eyes upon her.

"My lady," Bram replied as he bowed.

"Come, let's get ye inside," Rory said pulling her closer to him and heading towards the main entrance. "Ignore my brother. He is no' used to seeing me wit a lass."

"Have ye no' had many women?" she naively asked.

"Aye, but ne'er have I brought any of them home. Usually it's Bram flaunting the lasses around the keep. The mon can no' keep his hands from lifting skirts. Already he has two bastards living down here in the village. He is no' wit either of the women but he is good wit the bairns," Rory explained.

"Oh," she responded in surprise and looked back over her shoulder towards Bram.

The great hall was immaculate. The high walls were covered in the most beautiful tapestries Annella had ever seen. The floor was covered in fresh smelling rushes. The wood was polished and all of the candles in the room were lit. And there were several kitchen attendants and servants throughout the castle. It was obvious that what Rory had said about Lady Kenna was true; she took pride in making her castle very welcoming.

A young woman with black hair came up to greet them as they entered. "My Laird, it is good to see that ye have safely returned. I have just prepared the meal for the nooning and will be serving it shortly. I have been told that we have a guest that will be joining ye," the young woman said giving Annella a friendly smile.

"Elspeth, this is our future Lady of Dunakin, Lady Annella."

The look on Elspeth's face went flat and the color drained from her cheeks. Looking almost sickly, her eyes rolled back over to Annella. Feeling the intensity of her stare, Annella started to feel uneasy. Elspeth almost lost her footing when she quickly curtsied and spoke with a slight tremor, "My lady." Quickly she turned around and headed back into the kitchen as fast as her feet could carry her.

Annella cast Rory a puzzling look. Rory responded, "Ne'er mind her."

Knowing she acted so rudely for a reason, Annella wasn't about to let him brush it off as if it never happened. "What are ye no' telling me?"

Looking down at her, she could tell that he was not all too happy to discuss Elspeth. Taking a deep breath he said, "I dinna want to keep this from ye as I am certain ye will find out anyhow. Elspeth and I were once lovers. But that was a long time ago and there is nothing between us now. She is a servant who has been working in the kitchens for three years. Ye have nothing to worry about."

Lovers. Like hell she was going to allow his old lover to live in the same household as them. "She obviously dinna like me," she said crossing her arms.

"She does good work in the kitchens and kens what needs to be done around the keep, but I promise, if she causes ye any trouble I will have her gone."

"Alright," she agreed but wasn't too happy about succumbing so easily. She would have to keep an eye on that harlot.

Sitting at the head of the table, Rory watched as people joined in the festivity and merriment. Food and drinks were passed, stories were told by the men about the battle at Stirling and others danced around the room to the sound of the music the performers were playing. It was good to be home. He had announced to everyone that he and Annella would be joined in marriage in two days' time to allow Father Gregory to journey north from Buchannan Abbey.

Looking at her now, Annella looked amazed. Rory was concerned about his clan's behavior at first, as they could be rugged and not always well-mannered. But they, too, had impressed him. Annella seemed to look comfortable enough in her new surroundings as she spoke to some of the other women of the clan.

Leaning over to his brother, he quietly said under his breath, "Bram, ye and Ewan need to meet me in my solar. Dangers are afoot and we need to prepare the men."

"Ye brought the war home wit ye, aye?" Bram said looking both bothered and amused.

"It's a long story. One that needs to be discussed in private," he whispered.

Spinning in his chair, Rory faced Annella. "I need to discuss our situation wit the men and my brother. I will meet ye in our chamber tonight. My mother will take ye there. I apologize that I can no' show ye around properly but tomorrow I will give ye the tour."

"Our chamber? But I thought I would have my own," Annella interjected.

"My lady, we are to be husband and wife; ye will share my chamber. We will discuss this later." He didn't mean to sound so firm but there was no time to deliberate over it now.

Leaving the great hall, Rory was the last person to enter the library. Ewan, Bram and Colin all gathered around the desk waiting for him to enter.

"We apprised Bram of the situation," Ewan said as Rory sat down.

"Good. To my calculations, I would estimate that they will reach MacKinnon lands by this time tomorrow. I am no' sure if they are the English or that traitor Laird Stewart. According to Annella, he declares he will lay claim to MacCallum lands and is rightfully her husband. He had no proof to back his claim nor was the marriage consummated. My guess is that he comes for the lass. But he will no' be leaving here wit her."

"So ye did steal yerself a bride," Bram chuckled.

"If we have to fight, we will, to protect her, ye ken that," Colin said.

"Aye, I do. Tell the men to be on the lookout in the village. If they come for a battle, then a battle they shall have," Rory said with a wicked smile.

Annella watched Elspeth prance around the men as she cleaned off the tables. Occasionally she would glance over in Annella's direction and give her ill-mannered looks. Remembering what Rory had promised, she tried not to let it bother her. Elspeth was obviously feeling threatened by her presence. Perhaps if Elspeth got to know her better they could become friends.

Standing up from the table, Annella walked over to where Lady Kenna was sitting.

"My lady, I was told that ye can help me find my…I mean Laird Rory's chamber."

"Of course," she said kindly. "Follow me".

The chamber was located in the high tower. Annella could feel the cool draft coming from the windows as she passed them in the corridor. It reminded her of home. Feeling nervous, she wrung her hands together. The hallway was dark and alarming. At the end of the corridor stood a tall wooden door. Lady Kenna opened it and stepped inside.

As Annella entered, the dust from the room blew into her face. It was obvious that Rory had not been in his chamber in quite some time. She thanked Lady Kenna for her assistance.

"Have a good night, dear."

"Thank ye, ye as well," she said as she watched Lady Kenna close the door behind her.

Annella lit a taper that sat on a small round table by the door and glanced around the room. The dresser along the wall was made of hard wood and beautifully carved. An oversized bed was placed in the middle of the room. It had four large wooden posts on each of the four corners. The MacKinnon's red and green plaid laid on top. On the far end of the room stood a vast stone hearth. She wandered over to it and scanned the room for firewood. Spotting a small pile that was arranged next to the door, Annella picked up a few small logs. Placing them into the hearth, she took a flint from the table and lit the fire.

The light from the fire brightened up the room. Above the hearth hung a painting of an enchanting white castle. The picture was breathtaking. It reminded her of a place in a fairytale that her mother had once told her when she was just a bairn. She decided to lie down on the enormous bed, while nervously waiting for Rory.

By the time Rory came up to the room, the fire in the hearth was just about to die out. Deeply asleep in the middle of his bed was Annella cuddled up with his plaid. She looked so beautiful he thought. He slid off his boots and shirt and climbed into bed leaving on his trews. As he lay down, Annella rolled over and snuggled up against the crook of his arm. He wrapped his arms around her and closed his eyes.

"Good night, love," he whispered.

Annella quietly moaned in response but Rory was certain that she did not hear him.

Chapter 13

Annella awoke to find herself alone in Rory's oversized bed. Usually she was a light sleeper but it had been so long since she'd had a good night's sleep that she passed out as soon as her head hit the pillow and slept straight through the night. She wondered if she dreamt that she slept in Rory's arm or if he did hold her last night. After all, Rory did have a sneaky sense about him.

Sliding her legs over the side of the bed, they dangled several inches above the floor. She jumped down and went in search of her belongings.

"My lady, may I come in?" a voice called out from the other side of the door.

She went to open the door to see who it was. A young lass stood in front of her looking rather shy. With her head down, she softly spoke, "Good morning, my lady. My name is Muireal but ye can call me Lil. I am one of the maids that work within the castle and I have been asked to come and assist ye in getting dressed."

Lil reminded Annella of Caitlin back at Caerlaverock Castle. She had the same dull blondish hair and a mousy look to her. She couldn't help but wonder what would become of the lass who was once so kind to her.

Annella knew that she and Lil would become instant friends. Taking her hand, Annella guided Lil inside the chamber.

"Aye, please call me Annella. It is nice to meet ye, Lil."

"Oh nay, my lady. I can no' call ye that," she said looking shocked that she had received such a request.

"It's ok, ye dinna need to be so formal wit me. I am new here and I dinna ken anyone. It would be nice to have at least one friend." Annella smiled at her.

"A friend, my lady? I would like that verra much."

"Good, then it's settled. I was just about to clean up and don one of my dresses but because we left in such a hurry, I only had time to grab a few of them and these are in need of washing."

"Oh, my lady, if ye need a new dress, I can sew ye one. My momma taught me how to sew and I make all of my dresses," Lil perked up.

"That would be verra kind of ye, Lil. Thank ye."

She helped Annella into her red velvet dress and tied up the laces in the back while telling Annella all about herself. Once she opened up, Lil talked about her life here in the castle and all about the MacKinnon clan. Besides Lady Kenna, Lil had never been around another lady of her class. Lil was overjoyed having a new friend, as was Annella.

"Ye should go now into the great hall to break yer fast, Lady Annella. I am sure my Laird will be expecting ye."

"Aye, thank ye again, Lil. I look forward to seeing ye again."

Smiling back at her, Lil picked up the dirty dresses and led her to the great hall. She smiled and skipped off. She was excited to get started working on Annella's new gowns.

"Good morning, my lady," Rory said as he greeted her at the bottom of the stairs. "I see ye have met Lil."

"Oh aye, she is a sweet lass. I like her verra much."

"Aye that she is. Yer food has already been set on the table and after ye eat I shall take ye on a tour of my home as promised."

Together they walked over to the table and sat down in front of their plates. Elspeth came over to the table and set down a jug of fresh milk, trying to avoid eye contact with both Annella and Rory. Annella looked at her and inwardly laughed off her insolence. Looking down at her plate, she had never seen so much food in one sitting. She took nibbles of everything that was offered. The food wasn't like Cook's food back home; it was delicious and flavorful.

An assortment of fruit-filled rolls, small cuts of roasted lamb, figs, apples and warm buttery oatcakes that melted in her mouth covered Annella's plate. She was glad that this morning was not a day of fasting.

After she had finished and was satisfied with a full stomach, Rory held out his hand and they walked together around the inside and outside of the castle. She listened as he described each room and its history. She enjoyed his stories of when he was young and wild. Spending time with Rory alone was nice; it gave Annella a chance to get to know him better.

They passed by the training fields where Annella saw Rory's men training with their long bows.

Noticing her curious attention he asked, "Well my lady, how about it? Care to show off yer skills?"

Annella looked at him with enthusiasm on her face, "Ye will let me challenge yer men?"

"Aye," he said as they strolled down to the fields.

Annella could hardly contain her excitement. This would be the first time she had ever been allowed to participate in a real challenge. The men watched as they came into view.

"The lady wishes to challenge ye," Rory explained to his men.

The men stood there and looked around at each other. One of the men spoke out, "But my Laird, she is but a lass."

"Aye that she is," Rory said smiling.

"Where is the target?" she asked looking around.

"Ye see that mark several yards away? There is a torn piece of plaid hung onto that tree. That is yer target," Rory explained as he held out a bow and arrow to her.

Annella searched the trees and found the piece of cloth hanging high on a tree branch from a distance. One by one the men aimed for the strip of material but not one of them managed to hit it.

Annella raised the bow and notched the arrow into place. Breathing slowly she aligned her target into her line of sight. She stood there quietly feeling the breeze of the wind. She knew that the air had to be perfect. She imagined her arrow whizzing through the air, through the trees and hitting the cloth square in the center. She took a deep breath and held it as she gradually let go of the tip of the arrow.

She let out her breath and watched it fly into the air. Hearing the thud echo through the trees, a man yelled out, "She did it! The lass actually hit it!"

Pride warmed her heart. She glanced over at Rory who presented her with a wide smile. The rush of pride she felt was exhilarating. She had never felt anything like it before. The men stood quietly stunned in amazement.

"Congratulations, my lady," Rory said.

"Thank ye. I think it is now yer turn, my Laird. And dinna worry if ye are no' any good, practicing is how ye get good at it," Annella innocently reminded him.

Annella noticed the men looking over at Rory with their eyebrows pinched together in confusion. She thought maybe they didn't know that Rory was not good with a bow and felt bad for embarrassing him.

"Ye are right, my lady; it is only fair to take my turn as well," Rory said as he grabbed the bow. Looking around at his men, he didn't want to let them down but most importantly he didn't want to let Annella down. In fact was he was excellent at archery. He had only fibbed about his lack of skill to continue being close to Annella when they first met.

He raised the bow and contemplated whether he should hit the mark or miss it. He didn't want her to know that he'd lied so he pulled the string back and carelessly released it, purposely missing the target.

Knowing all too well that Rory was an excellent archer and would never have missed such a mark, Colin spoke up, "My Laird it must have been the wind, for I have ne'er seen ye mmm…"

Quickly interrupting Colin before he could finish Rory spit out, "Well, I guess my lady's skill has proven to best all of us, Colin. Ye and yer men should keep training or it will be Lady Annella who will be at the front line of our defenses."

"My lady, shall we continue our walk?"

She nodded her head and placed her hand on his arm. Together they walked down the cobblestone path.

"I will have to come up wit a prize for winning, my lady."

"I dinna need a prize, my Laird. Just allowing me the satisfaction is gratitude enough."

"Well then, if no' will ye at least accept this?" Rory asked as he bent down and picked up a white daisy from the ground and placed it behind her ear.

Annella blushed and felt shivers crawl down her spine as Rory stared deeply into her eyes.

Elspeth left the castle after the kitchen was cleaned and walked down to the village, carrying the bedding that needed to be washed. Before she could enter the washhouse to retrieve the soap, a heavy-set man snuck around the bushes along the tree line and forcefully grabbed her arm. Elspeth dropped the bedding she held in her arms and drew a deep breath to scream for help. But before she could make a sound, the man took his other hand and held it over her mouth, preventing her from screaming and drawing attention to them. She struggled against his hold as he dragged her into the woods.

Walking far enough away to ensure that her screams of help would not be heard, he released her.

"I demand to ken what is the meaning of this?" she hollered as the man released her. She looked around and six giant Highlanders towered over her and began to circle around her.

"Hello niece," Laird Stewart said as he revealed himself from behind one of the trees.

She quickly turned around and her eyes widened. "Uncle, what are ye doing here? And why are ye hiding out in the bushes? What is going on?" she looked at him curiously.

"I apologize for the manner in which you were brought here. It was safer this way for the both of us. I heard rumors that yer Laird has brought home a lass wit him. Is that true?"

"Aye, Lady Annella. They are to be married. Why?"

Rubbing his chin with his thumb and forefinger he stood there contemplating his plan.

"She is no' to be trusted, Elspeth. She is an imposter. She has pledged her allegiance to the English King. She is posing as a loyal Scottish rebel to help the English hunt down the Lairds and Earls who dinna follow the English king. And she has plans to have yer Laird killed. I have seen the English. They are camped out no' too far away from here."

"The English? I have heard they might have scouts in the area but I dinna ken why they would travel this far to the north."

"Ye see? The cunning whore has planned all of this. The English are coming to destroy this clan for refusing to pledge their loyalty to the English King. Yer Laird is to be hanged."

"I must warn him," she said in a panic.

"Nay, she will be expecting that. Nay, what ye need to do is bring the lass to me. I will protect the MacKinnon clan from her treachery. I have brought my men of arms in secret. We will imprison her and take her to Wallace himself where she can confess her sins. I am afraid that if ye tell yer Laird his life could be in danger. Now ye dinna want that, do ye?"

"Nay, of course not. Oh, thank ye, Uncle. I will see what I can do to bring her here into the open, alone. I will no' fail ye, Uncle."

"Good lass. Ye were always my favorite, Elspeth," he said as he patted her on the head and watched her run back toward the village.

Now that his bait was set, all he needed to do was wait and his whore of a wife would enter his trap.

"Yer home is charming and so vast. I dinna ken how I will possibly find my way around without getting lost," Annella said as she held Rory's arm while they walked across the footbridge and down into the gardens.

Rory chuckled.

"My lady, ye are so beautiful."

Annella looked down and felt her cheeks blushing again. Rory reached out and cupped her chin in his hand raising her head up so that he could look into her eyes.

"Why do ye look down when I say that?"

Annella shrugged her shoulders and gave him an innocent look from underneath her eyelashes.

"A fiery lass like ye should be bold and confident, my lady, and ken that she is beautiful."

Looking up at the sky the clouds were moving faster and had begun to darken. "We should head back inside, my lady. It looks like a storm is coming."

"When can we talk about the approaching threat of Stewart and the English coming our way? Rory, I want to fight wit ye. I ken ye want me out of harm's way but he killed my father and almost killed me. I dinna want ye to fight my battle, this is my fight."

"Ye are so brave, lass. And aye ye are right.
I want ye as far away from the fighting as possible.
My men can handle any threat that comes to our
gates. If Stewart comes for a fight, then we will give
him one. But ye must promise that ye will no' be
near the danger."

"What if I stay on top of the curtain wall wit
the other archers?"

Rory smiled down at her, "When the time
comes, we shall see how events unfold."

Annella started walking down the hallway
toward the direction of the stairs. She passed a small
corridor. From the corner of her eye, she saw a
glimmer of light coming from underneath a floor
board that caught her attention. She could hear
voices coming from a room below. She looked back
down the hallway to see if anyone was nearby.
Seeing no one in sight, she slipped into the dark
corridor to better hear what was being said.

Leaning against the cold wall, she closed her
eyes to help her concentrate. It was not a habit of
hers to eavesdrop but when she heard Rory's voice,
curiosity got the best of her. Rory was speaking
with someone. Ewan, perhaps.

"Rory, a messenger came this morning. He
said that his Laird demands the release of Lady
Annella. They are camped out a few miles away.

They say that if we hand her over, there will nay be an attack. They just want the lass. About three dozen of 'em. No' nearly enough for them to actually win in battle against us."

"Gather the men, we will surprise them in the woods at nightfall. They will no' be expecting us to attack during the night. Send the messenger back to give them my response. Tell them that Lady Annella is no' married to Laird Stewart and that she will no' be leaving Dunakin."

Annella heard Rory pound his fist on something hard making a loud thumping noise, causing her to flinch. She put her hand over her mouth keep quiet. She started trembling and her eyes filled with tears. *Nay. I will no' let Rory or his people die because of me. If that whoreson wants a war, then damn it he will have one.* Annella quietly left the corridor and ran to their chamber.

Annella knew what she needed to do. She needed to leave, to face Stewart alone. She snatched her bow and quiver and laced up her leather riding boots. She snuck down the stairs and around the corner, waiting for the right moment when she could slip past the guards and into the stable.

Walking back from the village, Elspeth saw Annella sneaking around the courtyard. Wondering what she was up to, she began to follow her. *Traitor*, Elspeth quietly spoke. How dare she come here, steal Rory from her and sacrifice her clan to the wolves. Elspeth was not going to let that happen. She thought that with no one around, this was the perfect opportunity to lead her into the woods as her uncle had demanded. Rory would be safe and she would be there for him to run to looking for comfort from the hurt and betrayal Annella had caused. Elspeth felt that she worked too hard for some wench to show up and ruin the chance of a life with Rory for her.

"My lady, is there something I can help ye with," Elspeth asked as she entered into the stable closely behind Annella.

Surprised by her approach, Annella quickly turned around and dropped the reins she was holding.

"Ach, ye surprised me. I was just checking on my horse to see how he fared."

Annella was unsure that she could trust the woman. She didn't want Elspeth telling Rory that she had been out here. If he knew, he would stop her from going, but this was something that Annella needed to do.

"Ye ken, my lady, word is that the English are hiding out in these verra woods. I heard they are camped out just south of here. Ye look like yer going to go riding. I was just worried about yer safety, my lady. The Laird has said that nobody is to leave the castle grounds," she said acting like she was deeply concerned.

If Annella was going to report back to the English, she was going to give her a false report to lead her directly into her uncle's hands instead.

South of the woods? Annella noted. As soon as she could take her leave of Elspeth, she would jump on Finlay's back and head in that direction as fast as she could.

"Thank ye for yer concern. But as I said I am just visiting my horse. I am used to riding him on a daily basis," she said and turned her attention back to the stallion and began rubbing him down.

"Verra good, my lady," Elspeth said as she walked away grinning, hoping that Annella would take her bait.

Once Annella was alone, she mounted Finlay. Covering herself with an old cloak she found hanging on a rusty hook, she headed out the gates and into the woods. Dressed similar to the other village folk, no one recognized her.

Chapter 14

Rory and the small band of warriors made it all the way to the peak of the mountain before they stopped. They hid behind the tall trees watching and waiting for the moon to rise high in the sky. They would use the darkness as an advantage. At the bottom of the hill, several English tents had been erected and several men of arms were standing guard around their campsite. Rory gave the signal and each man slowly descended down the hill in a widespread formation.

From the corner of his eye, Rory watched as an English soldier walked past. He jumped out from behind the tree and launched his full body at the soldier. Putting one hand over his captive's mouth with the other wrapped around his head, Rory swiftly jerked the soldier's head, breaking his neck. Without even a whisper, the man quietly fell to the ground.

From the other side of the camp, Rory heard shouts of alarm, causing him and his men to advance inside the tented area. Swinging his blade, Rory cut down five more of his enemies. It was all too easy.

"My Laird, we have tied up the rest of the prisoners but there was no' a sign of Stewart or his men. All of these men be English," Ewan said.

"Of course we are English, you filthy barbarians," one of the prisoners hollered as he struggled against his bindings.

Rory walked up to the man and pressed the tip of his sword against his throat.

"Where is yer Earl and Laird Stewart?" Rory demanded.

The man looked at him with disgust and spit at him.

"I said speak or I will cut out yer tongue, laddie. Dinna be testing me."

Hesitantly the man replied, "The Earl did not come with us. We joined Stewart's men because he said that he could track the girl into the Highlands. However that traitor and his men escaped us this morning and we haven't seen him since."

Where would he have gone? Rory's mind carefully considered the man's words as gut-wrenching panic began to set in; causing the hairs on his arms to rise. *It's a trap!* With him and his best men gone from the castle, the castle now had little protection behind its walls.

"Tie the prisoners together and bring 'em to the dungeon. We must hurry."

"What is it?" Ewan asked.

"The castle is nay safe."

Ewan knew exactly what Rory meant and secured the rope holding the prisoners. Leaving a few men behind to bring back the prisoners, Rory and the rest of them raced back to Dunakin as fast as they could.

Dashing through the gates into the bailey, Rory was thankful that everything looked to be normal but he knew how deceiving appearances could be.

"Close the gates. I want this place searched. Check every room if ye have to," Rory roared as his men looked at each other in confusion.

Rory ran into the keep and up the stairs to his room to make sure that Annella was asleep and safe in his bed. Ewan closely followed. When Rory opened the door however, there was no sign of her.

Spotting Lil down the hall he called out, "Lil, where is Lady Annella?"

"I dinna ken where she is, my Laird. I have nay seen her since this evening. I thought she was sleeping in her chamber."

"What do ye mean ye dinna ken where she is?" Rory hollered at Lil.

"My Laird, I saw her head up the stairs toward yer chamber after she returned with ye this afternoon but that was the last time I saw her."

Rory tried to remember the events after their walk. He knew he had gone into the library to speak with Ewan and his brother. *Could she have heard us talking?* Rory then looked over into the wardrobe and froze.

Noticing the change in his behavior, Ewan asked, "What is it?"

"Damn it…she's gone. How the hell did she get past the guards?"

Running down the stairs, Ewan ran after him and called out, "How do ye ken she is gone?"

"Her bow and quiver are missing. She must have heard us say that the English were here. She must have gone to surrender herself, that daft woman. She could nay have gotten far."

What could she be thinking? Rory's insides tightened with nervousness. If Stewart got his hands on her, he may never see her again. He could not let that happen. He almost lost her once; he would not lose her again.

Jumping onto the back of their horses, Ewan and Rory disappeared through the gates. Time was short; there was no time to gather the men to join them. Racing through the woods, he called out for Annella but there was no answer. He felt both anger and fear; a deadly combination.

Elspeth watched as Rory and Ewan rode off into the woods. Annella had headed south, just as she had anticipated. She inwardly smiled as she saw Rory and Ewan race in the opposite direction.

Stealing a horse from the stables when no one was watching, she headed in the direction her uncle was waiting. Since she was just an assistant worker in the kitchen, no one would notice her absence.

She quietly entered the woods and once out of sight, raced through the trees to find her uncle. When she got to his camp, she saw Annella tied to a tree with a gag in her mouth.

"Ah, Elspeth. Well done. Ye have made yer uncle verra proud," Stewart said grinning.

Uncle? Annella gave Elspeth a deadly stare. She wanted to yell and rip Elspeth's hair out for her deceit. She realized she had been purposely led her right into Stewart's lair. She'd known she couldn't trust that woman from the start. Angry with herself for failing for the ruse, she struggled to loosen her bindings but was unsuccessful.

"Will ye now be taking her to Wallace? I am sure that Laird MacKinnon will be verra grateful that ye unmasked this traitor for what she really is. Perhaps ye will be rewarded."

"Ah niece, trust me, I have my reward," he said as he walked over to Annella and licked the side of her cheek. Unable to stop him, Annella tried to turn her head away from him but, he forcefully held her head in place. She pulled on her ropes only causing them to bite harder into her skin.

"I will return now and tell Laird MacKinnon that ye have found a traitor in his midst and are leaving to seek justice," Elspeth said as she began to walk away.

"Grab her," Stewart said to his guard pointing in Elspeth's direction. "Sorry, lass. But I'm afraid ye will have to come wit us. Ye see lass, I have come for my wife, Annella. I was the one who led the English here. Following Wallace's foolish rebellion only gets ye killed and banished. The English may be ruthless, but if ye give yer vow to them, they are like yer own personal guard dogs. I was the one who helped them seize Annella's castle and kill her father. And now that we are married, her lands, title and coin are rightfully mine. So ye see, I can nay have ye going back to tell yer Laird where my men and I be. Ye too are now a traitor and it will be my hand that takes the life of Laird MacKinnon, nay the English."

"Nay I dinna believe it. Ye said...I thought... What have I done?" Elspeth shrieked in distress.

A tall guard standing behind the bushes seized Elspeth's hands and tied them together. Struggling to free herself, she fought off her captor and ran as fast as she could, dodging tree after tree. She felt awful. She had betrayed Rory as well as Annella. She had easily allowed her own uncle to trick her because of her jealousy. Now her uncle was going to kill both Annella and Rory and it was all her fault. She had to get back to the castle, to

warn Rory and beg for forgiveness before he fell
into Stewart's trap.

Behind her, she heard Annella yell out a
muffled scream. She turned, whipping her long
black hair around and saw her captor release an
arrow in her direction. When it hit its mark she
looked down at her stomach where the arrow had
struck all the way through her body and protruded
out the front. Elspeth fell to the ground.

"Nay," Annella cried out as she saw Elspeth
falter. Their eyes locked onto each other as if
Elspeth were asking for forgiveness.

"Ye four, make sure she is dead and bury
her body. We dinna want her to be discovered. The
rest of us are leaving. Meet us back at the Wild
Boars Inn. Make sure ye are nay followed."

"Aye, my Laird," the men replied in unison.

The night was getting colder as the hours
passed. Aside from the sound of the crunching
autumn leaves kicking up from under the horse's
hoofs, the woods were silent. Clouds moved in,
covering most of the moonlight. Rory was starting
to lose hope, but he was determined not to give up
on Annella. He knew that she could be in grave
danger.

"Rory, we have searched for hours. It is too dark out here to see anything," Ewan said feeling distressed that their search had come up empty.

"Ye can go back if ye want to, Ewan. I am going to find her."

Just as despair filled Rory's heart, he saw a small group of men in the distance holding onto a lit torch. Could he be that lucky? Quietly slowing their horses, Ewan and Rory watched the men as they were searching for something, or someone.

"What do ye suppose they are doing out here in the darkness?" Ewan whispered.

"I am nay sure. Let's get a closer look." Rory murmured in a soft voice.

Together they rode in silence trying to prevent the horses from making too much noise plodding across the littered forest floor. Rory could hear the men talking among themselves but they were too far for him to make out what they were saying. He slid off his horse and readied his sword as Ewan did the same.

"There she is," called out one of the men in a gruff voice.

"It's about time. We should have been back hours ago and me legs are killin' me," replied another.

Squinting his eyes, Rory looked down where the man was pointing the torch. He saw a young woman curled up on the ground with her hair all tousled around her face. *Annella?* Instantly he was enveloped with fear. He felt the color drain from his face and his hands began to shake; he was barely able to hold onto the hilt of his sword. He dropped down to the ground on one knee and rested his bowed head on his arm using his sword as support.

But his fear and anguish did not last long. His nose flared with every deep exhale. He raised his head and fixed his eyes on the men before him. They didn't know it but they were already dead. All thought left his mind. Instinctively, he grabbed his sword as he bolted out of hiding and sliced his nearest opponent.

Filled with rage and adrenaline, he fought the four men like a wild beast. Ewan stayed back knowing that it was vital to give Rory the space he needed, to prevent being struck accidently as Rory raged.

Eventually the bodies of all four men were scattered across the ground. Rory stood trying to control his breathing. Ewan watched as he ran over to Annella's limp body.

Ewan walked up next to him, placing his large hand on Rory's shoulder and squeezed it. Bending down, Ewan brushed the hair out of her face. Taken by surprise, he took in a sharp breath.

"Rory, it no' be Annella. 'Tis Elspeth."

"What?" Rory asked almost not comprehending the words. "Elspeth?"

Rory struggled to hold back tears as he felt his heart ache. He had never been so scared in his life. Not even death scared him.

"That means Annella is still out there," Rory said in relief.

Standing up, Ewan said, "Then let's go find her."

"Hold still, ye blasted wench," Stewart growled as he tightly held onto Annella in his arms while they rode together on his horse.

"Ye are hurtin' me," she cried out.

Annella shifted her weight back and forth, trying to get out of his grip. He squeezed tighter, hurting her stomach, making her nauseated. Trying to stay calm, she looked down and tried to control her breathing to rid herself of the nausea.

Unfamiliar with this area, she had no idea where they were or where they were going. She knew that they must have ridden for hours since the sun was beginning to peak on the horizon.

"Men. We will stop and make camp. We should be a good distance away from both MacKinnon and the English," Stewart pronounced and climbed down from his horse.

Forcefully grabbing onto Annella's waist, he dragged her off the horse and threw her over his shoulder. She kicked out her legs trying to break free, causing Stewart to drop her on the ground, hard.

"Do that again, bitch, and I will nay be so generous," Stewart threatened. "Tie her to that tree over there," he demanded.

Annella carefully watched the men around her. She felt foolish for being a captive twice now but knew that as long as she was here, Rory was safe. They had ridden far away from MacKinnon's land and Rory had no idea where she was. Elspeth was the only one who knew what really happened and she was already dead. Even though Elspeth betrayed her, Annella still felt sorry for the young woman. No one should be betrayed so cruelly by their own blood.

The men in Stewart's party were scraggly looking men. They didn't act like a group of Highlanders who had fought in battles before. Annella wondered if they were just hired thugs that Stewart had offered coin for their services. She mused that in the end Stewart would most likely not pay them anyway.

Stewart was talking quietly with one of them when he noticed her closely observing them. Abruptly ending his conversation he walked over to her and sat next to her on the ground.

"I have seen that look before, my lady. Ye will no' be escaping me this time. I see yer fear in yer eyes, yer anger. But like a wild mare, ye just need to be tamed," he goaded.

Grabbing her hair, he let the loose curls slide through his dirty fingers.

"Ye owe me, Annella. Ye are my wife and I will be takin' what is mine," he said smiling, revealing his yellow stained teeth and bad breath.

Stewart took a small dagger out from his boot and cut the rope tied to the tree. Picking Annella up, he carried her into a nearby tent while Annella squealed and tried to wriggle free of his hold.

Pushing her down onto the pallet of hay, he began to loosen his trews and started to lift the hem of her dress. Before he could assault her, Annella felt his weight abruptly lift off of her as he was tossed several feet away.

Rory's towering figure was standing over him, sword drawn.

"Get up and fight, ye bastard."

Stewart nervously looked around the tent wondering if he had time to call out to his men. Sliding his hand down the length of his leg, he pulled out the dagger from its sheath at the top of his boot and swung it towards Rory's calf. Jabbing it into the muscle, he released the small knife and crawled out of the tent.

"Rory. Oh my God, ye are hurt," Annella cried.

Rory grabbed the handle of the dagger and pulled it out of his leg. He winced at the sudden pain.

"I'm fine. Stay here and dinna leave this tent until I come for ye," Rory said in a stern voice and hobbled out the entrance of the tent.

"Stewart," Annella heard Rory roar from outside the tent.

She slipped out through the opening and took cover beyond the trees as she nervously watched. Her throat constricted when she saw the dead bodies lying on the ground that Ewan and Rory had killed. She feared the same fate for Rory and Ewan.

Rory saw Ewan fighting with two of the other men while he scanned the forest looking for the cowardly Laird who had run off. Spotting him just beyond the camp he made his way toward him. With a bloodthirsty look in his eyes, Rory stared Stewart down. As he got closer, they circled around, waiting for the other to strike.

"Ye are foolish, lad. Ye will no' win this," Stewart provoked as he progressed forward, drawing out his sword. "She is just a worthless whore. Lower yer weapon and I will nay kill ye. I will let ye go, but Annella is comin' wit me. She is mine."

"Yer wrong," Rory snarled.

Rory raised his sword overhead and swung its blade. Stewart jumped to the side barely missing the blade's sharp edge. Stewart attacked, thrusting his sword forward. Ducking to avoid the swing, Rory then skipped backwards blocking the blow. Whirling around each other in a battle dance, their blades locked as the metal crashed each sword against the other. Twisting and dodging each attack, Rory brought his foot up and kicked Stewart's side causing him to stumble.

Slashing his sword through the air, he nicked the side of Stewart's face, drawing blood. Stewart raised his hand to his cheek. Looking down at the blood smeared on his hand, he hissed. Roaring out in fury, he ran toward Rory swinging his sword from side to side aggressively.

Rory leaped out of the way, turned and kicked Stewart square in the gut causing him to fall backwards. Crashing onto the ground, Stewart had the wind knocked out of him as he landed hard on his back. Rory slumped and took in a deep breath. With his opponent temporarily immobile, he loosened his grip from his sword to relieve some of the pressure from his fighting arm.

Despite all of Rory's years of training and combat, he did the one thing that he knew never to do during a battle, he let himself get distracted. Foolishly, he turned his head towards Annella. He knew that she had disobeyed his order and left the protection of the tent.

Their eyes locked as if time stood still. He felt comforted for just that moment knowing that she was unharmed. Hours earlier he thought her dead. He could no longer imagine life without her in it.

The moment he took his eyes off his enemy, Stewart kicked his feet from under him and Rory went crashing down to the ground dropping his sword out of arm's reach.

Annella panicked and ran as fast as she could toward the horses. Scurrying to stand up, Stewart circled around Rory, positioning himself and held his sword high.

"As I said before, I always win," Stewart said with a scowl.

Face down in the dirt, Rory struggled to stay brave. He was not afraid to die. He prepared himself for the blow that was to come. The one mistake that would cost his life was his one reason for living, Annella.

Knowing this was his last and only chance, with as much emotion as he could gather, Rory yelled out, "Annella, I love ye."

Annella, stopped in her tracks. Hearing words that had never been spoken to her before from anyone other than her parents, strengthened her will and encouraged her to run harder and faster.

She grabbed her bow and arrows that Stewart had tied to the saddle bags. Notching the arrow in place, she pointed it at Stewart's heart and released it at the same moment his sword started roaring down upon Rory. Stewart was hit and faltered, becoming weak. The weight of the sword caused his arm to give out and the sword embedded itself in the ground, just grazing Rory's side. Stewart looked down at his chest and at the arrow which had struck him through the heart. Raising his head, he looked back up at Annella in the distance.

With fury blazing in her eyes, she choked down a sob as she roared, "That…was for my father."

With another arrow already notched in place, she pulled the string back as far as it would go.

"And this is for me, ye bastard!"

Releasing the arrow, it lodged in his throat. Stewart immediately fell backwards as blood poured out of his neck. She stood still, watching the blood pool onto the ground. She dropped her bow as Rory came to his knees and faced her. Running to him, she fell to her knees before him and wrapped her arms around him kissing him over and over.

"What were ye thinking, ye daft woman? I told ye to stay inside the tent. I could have lost ye."

"I am sorry. I had to. I love ye," she said looking up at him trying to stop the tears from streaming down her cheeks.

"I love ye too, lass. But please dinna ever do that again." Holding her head between his hands, he kissed her with as much passion and love as he could.

Clearing his throat to casually interrupt the couple, Ewan waited for their attention. Once Annella and Rory looked in his direction he said, "My Laird, my lady. I think 'tis best we get going. There is a wedding tomorrow and I think ye dinna want to be late in attendin'."

Rory and Annella looked at each other and smiled.

"Aye, he is right," Rory said.

Rory got off his knees and lifted Annella up into his arms. Guiding her onto his horse, he swung up behind her and gathered the reins. Holding her closely, he sped the horse back to the castle. Annella was satisfied that she finally had her revenge on Stewart and that she was in the arms of the man she loved and who loved her.

Chapter 15

Before the sun went down, everyone in the keep was preparing for tomorrow's big day. Cook was prepping food, Lil was decorating the church and even some of the men from the village were in the bailey tidying things up at Lil's request.

Walking arm in arm along the curtain wall, Annella and Rory sat down on the ledge and watched the sun set. The rays of oranges and reds peaking from the horizon lit the sky.

"Ye saved my life today."

"A woman can only try, my Laird."

"Well, I am grateful for your efforts."

Sneaking up behind them, Lady Kenna called out, "Rory, Annella, there ye are. I have been looking everywhere for ye. I have something to show ye, my lady and the groom should nay be wit his bride this night. I do believe the men in the great hall are looking for ye as well, Rory."

Rory lifted Annella's hand, bent over and put his lips upon the back of it. "I shall see ye tomorrow, my wee bride. I will be the mon standing at the altar," he whispered.

"Thank ye for telling me because I would have detested marrying yer brother," she jested.

Rory strolled into the great hall and spotted Bram and Ewan sitting down at the table drinking whiskey. He walked over to join them.

"It's about time ye showed yer face. We have been waiting for hours. Drink brother, for tomorrow ye shall be tied down to a wife," Bram joked as he handed Rory a mug of whiskey.

"Better he than I," Ewan boasted. "For I shall ne'er marry."

"Me neither. Far too many lasses to bed," Bram replied.

"Ye say that now, but ye just wait. Some lass will come along and knock both of ye on yer arses," Rory said smiling, taking a big swig.

"And where is yer bride-to-be this eve?" Bram asked.

"Lady Annella and our mother are up in her chamber doing whatever it is lasses do."

"Why are lasses always so concerned about their dresses when after the wedding, ye are just gonna rip them off 'em anyhow? It's what's under their skirts that matter," Ewan bragged to Bram.

Bram shrugged and replied, "I ne'er want to have to bed down only one lass, there are just too many to choose from to settle down wit a single one of 'em forever."

"Says the mon with two bastards already," Rory interjected.

"Hey, I love me bastards. They be good lads."

Both Rory and Ewan looked at each other and laughed.

"Annella, this was the dress I wore when I married Rory's father, God rest his soul," Lady Kenna said holding up a white satin dress and wiped a tear from her eye.

The collar was beautifully stitched with light blue flowers. The sleeves were long and were pointed at the tips, and lace and ribbon flowed down the back of the dress.

"Oh my lady, it is the loveliest dress I have e'er seen. Thank ye," Annella said with tears brimming her eyes.

"I have always wanted a daughter and now I will have one," Lady Kenna said as she helped Annella into the dress to see where it needed to be hemmed.

"Aye, ye look lovely, my lady," Lil said sitting quietly on the stool waiting to assist Lady Kenna.

Annella stood in front of the mirror and stared at herself in the white gown. She never would have thought to see herself in a wedding dress but meeting Rory had changed all of that. She had given him her whole heart.

She frowned at the knowledge that her father was not there to witness this occasion. Thinking back to what her father had told her the last time she saw him, she remembered he had given his approval for the marriage to Rory if Rory had ever proposed the idea. It made her chest warm with happiness knowing that she would have had his blessing. She slipped out of the dress and laid it over the chair for Lady Kenna and Lil to finish.

She laid down in the large bed, too excited and anxious to go to sleep. For it wasn't just the upcoming wedding that caused her nerves and stomach to tighten, it was her thoughts of the wedding night.

The morning was bright and clear. There was not a cloud in the sky. This was the day that every lass dreamt about; her wedding day. With her dress fitting snug and hair braided to one side, Annella was ready. Taking a deep breath, she made her way down the stairs to greet Alastair. He took her hand tenderly and placed it upon his arm, sensing her nervousness.

"Yer father would have been verra proud of ye, my lady."

"I ken," she smiled.

Slowly they walked together between the rows of people and chairs. Annella felt hundreds of pairs of eyes watching her. But all she could focus on was the one man standing at the altar. He was dressed in a white tunic and kilt and the MacKinnon medallion hung around his neck. His hair was slicked back and he wore a dashing smile. Their eyes never strayed from each other.

When Alastair and Annella reached the front of the room where Rory was standing, Alastair kissed her cheek and placed her hand into Rory's opened palm. Rory took her hand and walked with her the rest of the way to stand before the priest.

Father Gregory had a soft voice and his words were spoken beautifully. When Father addressed her and asked her if she took Rory as her husband from now until forever, she happily said, "I do."

The ceremony was short and sweet. As Father Gregory pronounced them husband and wife, the crowd began to cheer.

"To Laird and Lady MacKinnon."

Everyone gathered in the great hall for the reception, where the food and drink had already been set out on the tables. The candles were lit and flowers were displayed upon the hearth. Couples danced around to the music and everyone enjoyed the merriment.

As the guests slowly started to dwindle, Rory thanked the neighboring Lairds and guests for their attendance before their departure.

Rory looked over to his bonny bride. She looked like an angel in white. The dress she wore was tight fitting and he could see her curvy figure. The sight both aroused him and filled him with jealousy as other men could also clearly see each and every curve. He quickly walked over to stand next to her.

Staring into her golden hazel eyes, he leaned down and whispered in her ear, "Ye are the bonniest lass in the room, wife."

"And ye are the most handsome, husband."

"I think I need to take ye out of this dress."

"And leave our guests? Will that no' be rude, my Laird?" she teased.

Lightly nipping on her ear he said, "This is my wedding night, and I am Laird of this castle, so I may do whatever I like. And right now I would like to take my wife upstairs into our chamber and ravish her out of this dress."

"Well then, my Laird, as lady of the castle what will ye do if I protest?" she taunted.

Playing into her game, Rory picked her up over his shoulder and started heading out of the great hall. The crowd of people laughed and teased as they watched Rory take off with his bride in a display of manliness as she demanded to be put down. Carrying her all the way up the stairs and into their room, he plopped her down onto the bed.

"Well, now that ye have me in here, what are ye going to do?" she taunted him.

"I'm gonna make love to ye, lass, until the sun rises in the morning."

He crawled up onto the bed and adjusted himself so that he could wrap both arms around her.

He pressed his lips hard to hers and greedily swept his tongue inside her mouth as he drew his hand up to cup one of her tantalizing globes. Her breasts were round and perky under his touch.

Rory began to smooth his hand down the side of her body. He sat back on his heels and placed his hands just above her knees and leisurely hiked up her dress over her thighs.

Annella froze for a moment from the contact of his hand on her thigh and let out a quick breath. She felt the wetness between her legs and unconsciously began to raise her hips and spread her legs open a little wider.

"I ken ye are nervous, but I will nay hurt ye. Do ye trust me?" Rory asked.

"Aye," she softly replied

He glided his hand upward until he got to the apex of her thighs. With his index finger he found her sensitive pearl and slightly pressed down and massaged it, causing Annella to whimper and mutter. He leaned forward kissing the side of her neck. He lingered there for a few moments licking and nibbling on her flesh. With one daring move, he placed a finger onto the soft creamy folds.

"Ye are so wet," he lightly said in her ear. Then he pushed his finger inside of her. Annella suddenly lifted her head and cried out.

Rory slid his finger back out and continued to gently increase the speed and momentum.

"Oh my, Oh Rory," she moaned not wanting him to stop. The pressure in her body was building up and she was just beginning to feel the release.

"That's it, lass. Let me hear ye," he encouraged.

Annella's lips parted and she suddenly felt an explosion of emotion as tremors shattered though her body and she hit her climax. She tried to steady her breathing, indulging in her new found feeling. She wanted more of him, all of him. She wanted to feel his bare hands upon her skin and to touch him as well.

Shamelessly she grabbed at the laces of her dress and began to loosen them. Letting the dress drop from her shoulders and pool around her waist she sat there with her breasts exposed. Rory leaned in and took one of them into his mouth. Annella combed her fingers through his hair pressing his head closer to her chest.

She scooted up further onto the bed, removing her dress completely. She grabbed onto the bottom of Rory's tunic and began to lift it up over his head. Spreading her hand on his chest, she glided her fingers downwards to his stomach. His muscles were ribbed and hard to the touch, but his skin was soft and warm.

She laid back so her head hit the pillow as Rory followed. He removed the pin that was holding his kilt in place and kicked it off onto the floor. Lying side by side fully exposed, she could feel the heat radiating off his body. Annella leaned up and kissed him fervently, letting her hands explore his body.

Annella stopped at the sight of Rory's enlarged swollen appendage sticking out and swallowed hard.

"Is everythin' alright?"

"I'm afraid it may no' fit and will hurt."

Rory chuckled a little but realized that by doing so, he may inadvertently hurt her feelings. He had always been with common barmaids and whores but never a virgin lass. "Dinna be afraid, love, trust me it will fit."

Wanting to know how it felt, she cautiously lowered her hand towards it and lightly touched the tip. Rory moaned. She ran her fingers up and down the length of the shaft and smiled at the funny facial expressions Rory had upon his face.

"If ye keep doing that lass, it will be over before we e'en get started."

Annella giggled.

Positioning himself over her, he rested himself between her legs, keeping his weight on his elbows.

"This will hurt but only for a wee bit. The pain does go away. I promise."

Annella felt her body quiver with anticipation. Pressing the tip against her folds, he pushed forward with one hard thrust and broke through her maidenhood. He laid there motionless, allowing her pain to ease.

Annella cried out. Both arms wrapped tightly around Rory's neck.

"I'm sorry, lass. I ken it hurts but only the first time and it will no' hurt for much longer."

Taking a deep breath, she replied, "The pain is starting to go away."

She lifted her hold from around his neck, slid her hands down his back and stopped at his hips. She began to slowly grind her hips up and down. Rory pulled out a little and pushed back in matching her tempo.

"Oh Rory," she bellowed and encouraged him to go faster.

With no argument, Rory moved his hips faster and harder wanting to be completely inside of her. She felt so good. He knew that he wouldn't be able to control himself much longer. Not wanting to slow down, his kisses became more aggressive and demanding.

"Ye are mine. Always," Rory said in between his passionate kisses and thrusts.

"Always."

Annella held onto Rory as tight as she could. Her body tingled all over. As she felt the increased sensation, she knew she was on the verge of climaxing again. Yelling out Rory's name, she felt the eruption throughout her body. At the same time, she felt Rory's body shudder as he emptied his seed inside of her.

With sweat rolling down his face and heavy breaths, Rory tried to steady himself. He could lay in Annella's arms forever. He had never felt this way with anyone before. He pulled the plaid over them and snuggled up behind her. Holding her in his arms, he applied soft kisses to the back of her neck. Annella was in awe of what she felt.

"I could ne'er get enough of ye, lass. I want ye again."

Cradling her head in the crook of his arm, Annella closed her eyes and smiled for she knew what it meant to love and be loved in return.

The End.

Author's notes:

Thank you for reading. If you enjoyed this book, please consider reading Book 2: *Escape to the Highlands,* a continuation of Ewan's story.

Escape to the Highlands:

Her enemy was the only one she could trust...

Jacqueline Renold, an English born lady is the sister to the king's executioner. In love with one man and forced to marry another, she feels no different than the prisoners below in the dungeons. After witnessing one too many Scots hung by the noose, she makes a decision that would change her life, she frees the prisoners. Knowing her actions are treason, she flees to Scotland with a bounty on her head...

Ewan, the Laird's cousin is second in command of their army. Third in line to the MacKinnon Clan, he has no home or land of his own, only the sword on his back. Through his skill as a warrior, he seeks out to find his place in the world. Ewan travels south with William Wallace to help free those who the English have been taken captive. But when duty and honor leads Ewan to help an English lass in grave danger, the last thing he expects is to lose his heart to his enemy.

About the Author

April lives in Minnesota with her husband and they are expecting their first child March 2014. April developed her passion of historical romances from her love of history and genealogy. Over the last several years she has completed her family tree finding over 350 bloodline grandparents dating back to the 1100s.

For more information about April and her upcoming books please follow her at:

www.facebook.com/author.april.holthaus

Made in the USA
Charleston, SC
10 January 2015